THE
GOLDEN
SWIFT

BY LEV GROSSMAN

★

THE SILVER ARROW SERIES

The Silver Arrow

The Golden Swift

THE
GOLDEN
SWIFT

Lev Grossman

ILLUSTRATED BY Tracy Nishimura Bishop

LITTLE, BROWN AND COMPANY
New York Boston

Copyright © 2022 by Cozy Horse Limited
Interior illustrations by Tracy Nishimura Bishop

Cover art by Brandon Dorman. Cover design by Sasha Illingworth. Cover copyright © 2022 by Hachette Book Group, Inc.

Little, Brown and Company
Hachette Book Group
1290 Avenue of the Americas, New York, NY 10104
Visit us at LBYR.com

First Edition: May 2022

Little, Brown and Company is a division of Hachette Book Group, Inc. The Little, Brown name and logo are trademarks of Hachette Book Group, Inc.

The publisher is not responsible for websites (or their content) that are not owned by the publisher.

Library of Congress Cataloging-in-Publication Data
Names: Grossman, Lev, author. | Bishop, Tracy Nishimura, illustrator.
Title: The Golden Swift / by Lev Grossman ; illustrated by Tracy
   Nishimura Bishop.
Description: First edition. | New York : Little, Brown and Company,
   2022. | Series: The Silver Arrow | Audience: Ages 8–12 | Summary:
   Kate and Tom are now full-fledged conductors of the steam-powered,
   animal-saving Great Secret Intercontinental Railway, but when Kate
   takes the *Silver Arrow* out on an unsanctioned mission to find Uncle
   Herbert she discovers a mysterious train called the *Golden Swift* with an
   agenda of its own.
Identifiers: LCCN 2021062035 | ISBN 9780316283540 (hardcover) |
   ISBN 9780316283861 (ebook)
Subjects: CYAC: Locomotives—Fiction. | Railroad trains—Fiction. |
   Adventure and adventurers—Fiction. | Magic—Fiction. | Brothers and
   sisters—Fiction. | LCGFT: Action and adventure fiction. | Fantasy
   fiction. | Novels.
Classification: LCC PZ7.1.G785 Go 2022 | DDC [Fic]—dc23
LC record available at https://lccn.loc.gov/2021062035

ISBNs: 978-0-316-28354-0 (hardcover), 978-0-316-28386-1 (ebook)

Printed in the United States of America

LSC-C

Printing 1, 2022

⭐

FOR ROSS, HALLY AND BAZ

The Way Things Are Done

THERE'S A WAY THINGS ARE DONE, AND THIS IS NOT IT.

I didn't come up with it, Kate thought. *I don't even like their stupid way! But if they came up with it, they should stick to it.*

Kate didn't say any of this out loud—she often felt like she delivered her best speeches in her head, where they didn't receive the popular acclaim they deserved. She was standing on a cold, rainy sidewalk in downtown Chicago in front of a skyscraper, one of those extremely tall and skinny and futuristic sky-scrapers that are the native habitat of the common billionaire.

"Let's go, Kate. He's not here." Her mother was wet and exasperated and generally over it all. "Typical Herbert!"

Kate couldn't really disagree on either point. This was definitely Uncle Herbert's address, but the man at the front desk equally definitely said he'd never heard of him. If Uncle Herbert was here, then it wasn't in any visible or otherwise detectable form.

And also it really was typical Uncle Herbert.

Kate had only just met her uncle for the first time last year, and on the whole it had been a pretty good year since then. On her eleventh birthday, which had ended up lasting for several weeks, Herbert—who was in fact a billionaire—and also it turned out a wizard—had given Kate a steam train called the *Silver Arrow*. The *Silver Arrow* was a magic train that had a candy car, and a library car, and an unbelievably cozy sleeper car. It was part of a vast invisible worldwide train service dedicated to helping animals in need, which there seemed to be more and more of lately.

Oh, and the animals could talk. And the *Silver Arrow* could talk, too. This whole story was so flagrantly implausible that Kate had already resigned herself to never telling it to anybody; she guessed she could file it away with all those great speeches she made in her head that nobody would ever hear. At the end of their first trip, Kate and her younger brother, Tom, were made official conductors of the Great Secret Intercontinental Railway.

But it wasn't one of those adventures that happens once and then you have to remember and savor and treasure it for the rest of your otherwise uneventful life. Since her birthday, Kate and Tom had gone on about a dozen trips on the *Silver Arrow*. At first she'd tried to keep a journal of them, but that had lasted about a trip and a half before she got lazy about it, and then some rabbits ate it, so that was that. She guessed she just wasn't a journal-keeping person.

But she'd helped hundreds of animals get where they needed to go, or get away from whatever they needed to get away from, or find whomever or whatever they were looking for. She'd ridden the *Silver Arrow* down deep tunnels, across luminous blue glacier crevasses, past secret vine-covered temples deep in sweltering equatorial rain forests.

It was everything she'd always been looking for without even knowing she was looking for it. Kate had always thought of herself as the kind of person who would one day lead a secret double life, and she'd figured her second life would probably be something in the superhero or espionage line, rather than the secret-invisible-train-conductor line. But she couldn't have been happier with how things had turned out.

Or not literally. She could actually have been a little bit happier. Kate wasn't complaining—it had been drummed into her in Social and Emotional Learning class that complaining was not a productive way to deal with personal challenges, and she figured her Social and Emotional Learning teacher had probably had her share of personal challenges since her name was Ms. Tinkler.

But if Kate were going to complain, just hypothetically, her complaints would have been as follows. There were five of them.

Complaint number one: Leading a double life was nowhere near as easy as it looked. Before all this happened she hadn't even been that good at leading one life, and now that she had two they had a way of getting tangled up with each other. Problems from one life had a way of following you into the other one and vice versa. For example, Kate was always worrying about a social studies quiz when she should've been rescuing a sugar glider from a bushfire in Australia, and then in class when she was trying to remember the cause of the French Revolution (it was poverty), her brain would suddenly choose to worry about how chimney swifts were running out of chimneys to build their nests in.

And what was even the point of leading a double life if you couldn't use one to run away from the other?

Complaint number two: Tom. Unbelievably, Tom had been showing signs of not being quite as interested in the *Silver Arrow* as he used to be. In fact he'd skipped the last couple of trips, which she found

completely unacceptable on any number of levels.
Kate would never dream of missing a chance to ride
the *Silver Arrow*!

But Tom was nine now and big for his age, and
he was getting really, really into hapkido, to the point

where he'd been saying he
didn't have time for the
Silver Arrow. Which Kate
pointed out made no sense,
because magical trips on
the *Silver Arrow* took no
time at all. But then he
just said he was "tired,"
and what could you say
to that?

Admittedly, he was
getting pretty good at
hapkido. Tom was an
upper blue belt now, and they
were letting him use the nunchucks, and not just
to fool around with but to actually hit people. And
they hurt, as she found out when he hit her with
one, which, yes, she had invited him to do, but
only because she'd always thought they were just

toys! Regardless: Kate couldn't understand what he could possibly be getting out of hapkido that would be more important than the *Silver Arrow*. And she hated that. And she hated not being able to understand her own brother.

Complaint three was that she lost out on the part she wanted in the school musical, namely beguiling young heiress Hope Harcourt in *Anything Goes*. She got put in the chorus instead. And she couldn't quit now because she'd look like a sore loser. And she was a sore loser! But she didn't want to *look* like one.

That had nothing to do with the *Silver Arrow*, but she was still annoyed about it, so she put it on the list.

Four was that as hard as she worked on the *Silver Arrow*, as many animals as she helped, as hard as she tried, it was never, ever enough. There were always more animals in trouble. Kate read a lot, and in her experience stories with magic in them usually ended up with the world being saved at the end. But this was different. Kate tried and tried, and was brave, and never gave up, and generally acted like a hero, and *still* the world wasn't saved.

She'd developed an unhealthy obsession with the bushfires that were raging in Australia, and she kept scanning news stories for the names of more and more obscure, irreplaceable little animals that were now being threatened with extinction—not just koalas and wallabies but numbats, and quokkas, and dunnarts. She'd never even heard of a dunnart, which was apparently some kind of tiny furry marsupial that looked exactly like a mouse, and of which there were no fewer than nineteen species, from the slender-tailed dunnart to the lesser hairy-footed dunnart. And now they were going extinct!

She felt so hopeless. When she went on her first mission on the *Silver Arrow* she thought she might actually make things better and bring some balance back to the world, but things had only gotten worse and worse. Adults—her parents, her teachers, the president—always talked about how *concerned* they were about the environment, what a terribly urgent *crisis* it was, but none of them ever seemed to do anything about it, and meanwhile every time Kate saw something in the news about ice caps melting or rain forests being cut down or bees disappearing, she thought of her friends, like the white-bellied heron, and the fishing cat, and the polar bear, and she had to leave the room so no one would ask her why she was crying.

And finally, complaint number five was that she couldn't even go out on the *Silver Arrow* anymore because Uncle Herbert had disappeared! He was the one who gave Kate her missions. That was how things were done. But she hadn't seen him for two months, and no one—not Tom, not their parents, not the *Silver Arrow*, not the porcupine who lived in the woods behind her house—had any idea what had happened to him.

Which meant that it was up to Kate to find him. She would've preferred to spend this particular rainy weekend curled up indoors with a book, or making origami boxes out of fancy paper, or drawing exotic flowers from photos she found on the internet, instead of traipsing—traipsing!—around Chicago in the freezing rain in search of her feckless billionaire uncle.

But no one else was going to do it, so it was up to Kate to solve the problem. Because that, all too often, was the way things were done.

The Board of Directors

CLICK-*BING*.

THERE'S A WAY THINGS ARE DONE

AND THIS IS NOT IT

"I know that! Believe me! I know how things are supposed to be done!"

Kate couldn't believe a talking train was stealing her private mental speech.

THEN WHY ARE YOU DOING THINGS IN A WAY THAT IS NOT THAT WAY

"Because the way things are done isn't working! So. We're going to make up our own way."

Kate was crouched in the cab of the *Silver Arrow*, sweating from the heat, her knees aching, as she scraped and shoved around inside its firebox with a ridiculously long-handled rake to try to get the fire going. It was hard work, and it wasn't helping that the *Silver Arrow* was giving her a hard time while she did it.

Tom wasn't helping, either. He was standing on one foot on the engine's giant boiler, practicing his balance. It was a hapkido thing.

The problem was that they didn't have a time-table. Herbert was supposed to turn up at their house once every few weeks to drop one off. He was getting along better with Kate's parents these days—he was even getting them more interested in the environment. Kate's parents had wanted to sell off the parcel of woods behind their house, but Herbert convinced them to try "rewilding" it instead. *Rewilding* meant leaving the land alone and letting it go back to its natural state. There was an endangered dragonfly called a Hine's emerald that used to live in the area, and Kate's mom was hoping that if they rewilded their land enough, it would come back. Kate suspected that this was a high-minded scheme whereby her parents could congratulate themselves for not mowing the lawn—and there was some loose talk about "making a small fortune" from "ecotourism"—but in theory she guessed she was in favor of it.

After Herbert's visits Kate would always find a piece of paper in her room, hidden somewhere weird like under her mattress or rolled up in one of her socks or plastered inside a lampshade. It was high-quality paper, creamy and thick, the kind of paper you'd expect to find a royal proclamation or a doctorate in physics printed on.

But instead it would be a train schedule. It looked something like this:

THE GREAT SECRET INTERCONTINENTAL RAILWAY
OFFICIAL TIMETABLE
for
THE SILVER ARROW

Serving distressed, displaced, and otherwise imperiled animals

MAKING THE FOLLOWING STOPS AT THE FOLLOWING TIMES:

Daintree Rain Forest, Australia	4:33 p.m., February 22
East Siberian Taiga, Russia	2:30 p.m., February 22
Sinharaja Forest Reserve, Sri Lanka	7:12 a.m., February 22
Carcross Desert, Canada	6:41 a.m., February 22
Western Ghats, India	8:57 a.m., February 22
Xishuangbanna Rain Forest, China	12:02 a.m., February 22
Maluku Islands, Indonesia	3:11 p.m., February 22
Mt. Baker-Snoqualmie National Forest, United States	1:19 p.m., February 22

And so on. The stops were always all on the same day, which made no sense, and they weren't even in chronological order, or anywhere near one another, but that was the GSIR for you. Making sense was not on the agenda. On the appointed day Kate would build up the fire in the *Silver Arrow*, and lubricate its various bits that needed lubricating, and polish the bits that weren't already blindingly bright and shining, and off they would go.

But without a timetable, they couldn't go anywhere. And without Herbert, there were no timetables.

"Ergo," Kate concluded, "we have to go and rescue Herbert."

The fire was finally catching, and the cab filled with the familiar savory smell of mingled wood and coal smoke.

YOU HAVE TO GO AND RESCUE HERBERT

"I tried. Want to know how hard I tried? First I Googled 'Uncle Herbert.' Then I snuck my mom's credit card out of her purse and used it to pay $4.99 for a public records search to find his address, which probably wouldn't have worked if he didn't have a weird last name, but he does, and I got an address for him.

"Then I used my mom's credit card to order a book about lemurs."

HOW DID THAT LAST PART HELP?

"It didn't. I just wanted a book about lemurs."

BETTER TO ASK FORGIVENESS THAN PERMISSION

"Exactly. Then I told my mom we were going to surprise Uncle Herbert with a visit, so we went all the way into the city to the address I found, but when we got there, he wasn't there. They didn't even know who he was. That's as far as I got on my own. So now you and I are going to go find him."

HOW DO YOU EVEN KNOW HE NEEDS RESCUING

MAYBE HE'S JUST TAKING A WELL–DESERVED VACATION

"He doesn't deserve a vacation. He deserves a kick in the butt."

WHAT IS HERBERT'S WEIRD LAST NAME

"Yastremszki. It's my mom's maiden name. Any other questions?"

Kate closed the door to the *Silver Arrow*'s firebox with only a little more force than was strictly necessary and started checking half a dozen gauges.

WE CAN'T TRAVEL WITHOUT A TIMETABLE

THE RISKS WOULD BE UNACCEPTABLE

"I accept the risks," Kate said. "See? I just accepted them. *Ergo*, they are acceptable."

I DON'T KNOW WHAT *ERGO* MEANS

"Well, I feel sorry for you."

I DON'T THINK YOU KNOW WHAT *ERGO* MEANS EITHER

"Of course I— Wait. What exactly are the risks?"

I'LL TELL YOU WHAT THEY ARE

WITHOUT A TIMETABLE WE COULD RUN OUT OF COAL

WE COULD RUN OUT OF WATER

WE COULD COLLIDE WITH ANOTHER TRAIN

WE COULD ENCOUNTER A TRACK OUTAGE

**IF WE GET IN TROUBLE NOBODY KNOWS WHERE
WE ARE**

AND LAST BUT NOT LEAST

**WE WOULD INCUR THE WRATH OF THE POWERS
THAT BE**

"Interesting. Who are the powers that be?"

Kate had always wondered who was actually in charge of the Great Secret Intercontinental Railway, but Herbert would never give her a straight answer about it.

THE BOARD OF DIRECTORS

"Well, the Board of Directors has incurred *my* wrath. Ever think of that?"

YES I DID THINK OF THAT

Kate had had enough of this argument. If it went on much longer, the *Silver Arrow* was going to win it. So instead of answering, she released the brakes.

Kate still got a thrill whenever she did that. Something about the deep, satisfying *snap* it made—she'd read somewhere that when sperm whales do echolocation they make a deep *click* sound, like a bat's squeak, except so loud that if you were a diver underwater and a sperm whale *click*ed at you, you would feel the sound resonate all the way through you, right to the core of your being. That's what the snap of the *Silver Arrow*'s brakes felt like to Kate. The train began rolling smoothly forward, all 102.36 tons of it, with the precision and delicacy of a cue ball across a pool table.

Tom yelped and dropped his hapkido pose and came scrambling back inside.

WAIT WAIT WAIT WAIT!

"For what?"

WE WEREN'T DONE ARGUING!

"I was done. There are animals all over the world that could die without our help. I'm not going to sit around on my duff any longer not helping them."

She eased out the throttle. From somewhere the *Silver Arrow* emitted a hiss of steam that sounded suspiciously like a sigh.

THIS IS ABOUT THE PLAY

ISN'T IT

Kate's hand was steady on the reverser as they made the sharp turn past the Achebes' house and into the damp cold April woods.

"It's not about the play."

It Was a Little
Bit About the Play

LOOKING BACK, KATE COULDN'T EVEN REALLY SAY WHY she thought she'd get the part. She'd never thought of herself as a drama person before. Or a singing person, either.

Last year, when she was still in elementary school, she'd gone to see the middle school musical, which was *Into the Woods*. She'd been so swept away that she went back again the next night. It just looked so *fun*. Everybody looked so confident and grown-up and romantic and happy. They looked like they knew who they were and where they belonged, in a warm, glowing world full of hilariously complicated problems that somehow all worked out all right in the end.

So this year when she saw the poster announcing auditions for *Anything Goes*, Kate signed up immediately. It wasn't even a decision. She knew exactly which part she wanted, namely Hope Harcourt, beguiling young heiress.

Part of it was that she was at a new school, and she was still trying to figure out where she fit in. In elementary school she'd always been looking for her thing, her talent—something, anything, that she was good at, that would make her special. And she'd finally found it—boy, had she found it—but then the irony was that she couldn't tell anybody about it!

So fat lot of good that did. To everybody else she just looked as plain and ordinary as she always had.

Plus she felt like she'd outgrown her old elementary school friends, and she somehow hadn't managed to find any new friends to replace them with. She wondered sometimes if it wasn't just a tiny bit the *Silver Arrow*'s fault—if spending so much time talking to a steam train and saving animals made it harder to relate to her classmates who led normal lives.

But that's where the musical came in. Being Hope

Harcourt would be like being the conductor on the *Silver Arrow* only everybody would know about it, and they'd be in it with her. And at the end of the show when Hope Harcourt had her happy ending, it would stay that way. She felt guilty about wanting a life apart from the *Silver Arrow*, but wasn't everybody entitled to their own life? And to friends who weren't a magic steam train? She was eleven going on twelve. Sometimes you just need somebody to talk about cat stickers with.

There was just the little business of actually getting the part.

Obviously, you had to sing a song at the tryouts, and Kate had basically never sung anything in her life except Christmas carols and "Happy Birthday." She wasn't going to sing "Happy Birthday" at her audition, so she went with "Silent Night." There was no way she was going to sing in front of Tom, or her parents, or her uncle, or her friends, so she practiced in secret, picking out the notes on their piano to make sure she was on pitch.

Or more or less on pitch. Sometimes it was hard to tell. "How are you going to get up and sing in front of Mr. Lee and all the other kids if you can't sing in front of your family?" Uncle Herbert asked her on one of his visits. It was one of those questions that's so reasonable and sensible that the only thing you can do is pretend you didn't hear it.

Tom would never have had a problem with this. He was always walking around rapping and singing pop songs at the top of his lungs. He *liked* people hearing him! Stuff like that just came naturally to him.

The auditions were held in the auditorium, the same one where she'd seen *Into the Woods* last year. At night it had seemed glamorous, but now in the daytime it was just big and empty and echoey. The chairs were those wooden ones where when you stood up, the seat automatically bounced up on a spring and made a huge bang. She recognized a few of the kids who'd been in the show last year, and they were funny and relaxed and confident, just like they had been onstage. They laughed and joked with each other and Mr. Lee as if they were still in the musical and somebody had written witty lines for them to say.

Mr. Lee called the auditioners up to the front one by one. A tall, willowy girl belted out a song called "The Ladies Who Lunch" with a lot of funny facial expressions and grown-up-sounding jokes that Kate didn't get. Her voice had that vibrato thing that real singers have. Kate didn't think she sounded like that. Though you could never tell. She'd read somewhere that you could never really hear what your own voice sounded like, because the sound was transmitted to your ears through your jawbones, or something like that. So maybe she sounded like that and she just didn't know it.

A few of the kids tried to sing pop songs but cracked up in the middle. A couple more really did sing "Happy Birthday." (Valuable life lesson: The first note of "Happy Birthday" is the lowest note in the song, it only goes up from there, so if you start too high you'll end up squeaking at the top.) Two unbelievably good-looking eighth graders did a duet from *Frozen*, complete with little snippets of funny dialogue that sounded exactly like the movie, and they sang actual harmony together in the chorus. A girl who Kate had seen around since kindergarten but never talked to, and who she'd always felt bad for because she was so shy, got up and without a hint of nerves belted out a song from *Dear Evan Hansen*, and her voice was like an opera singer's. When she was done, the whole auditorium applauded.

By the time Mr. Lee called Kate's name, it had crossed her mind that she might be making a mistake, but by then it was far, far too late. And in stories isn't it exactly the girl who thinks she could never be a star who always ends up *being* the big star and is showered with flowers and confetti while she stands there saying, *Who, me?*

She really hoped that that was what was going on here. Because it was definitely how she felt.

But in those stories did it feel like you were on the moon as you climbed the stairs up to the stage? Did your legs feel like numb stilts, and did your scalp start prickling with itchy sweat? The auditorium went quiet around Kate except for tiny noises that suddenly sounded incredibly loud, and Mr. Lee's smile as he asked her what she was going to sing was so kindly that it made her want to cry. And how exactly did your vocal cords work, again? Because it had gone clean out of her head. Mr. Lee had to sing the first few notes of "Silent Night" for her to get her started.

When she was done she ran back to her seat, her face glowing with embarrassment.

That was on a Monday. On Thursday morning when she got to school, the cast list was up, and there was a mob of kids already gathered around it, buzzing and chattering away excitedly about who got what part. She waited on the edge of the crowd for a while, listening. What was that they were saying? Were they saying, *Who is that unknown sixth grader who came out of absolutely nowhere to capture the coveted role of Hope Harcourt, the beguiling young heiress who gets to sing "It's De-Lovely" with brash young stowaway Billy Crocker?*

Nope. They were not.

There were two names next to each of the lead roles so that different kids could play them in the

Friday- and Saturday-night performances. But Kate would not be playing Hope Harcourt on either night. She got put in the chorus, with the failed pop-song kids and the "Happy Birthday" kids.

Kate spent the rest of the day in a swamp of embarrassment and shame. *How* could she have done it? *Why* had she ever thought that she was special or talented in any way? She was too embarrassed to even talk to anybody about it; when her parents asked how it went, she just pretended, not very convincingly, that it wasn't a big deal. The only one she told her real feelings to was her magic steam train friend, the *Silver Arrow*, which tried its best to sympathize, but let's face it, her problems were somewhat outside its experience.

Of all the many aspects of this unfortunate situation

that she might have obsessed over, for some reason one in particular tormented her more than the others.

After she'd run back to her seat, her face as red as a baboon's bum, a boy she'd never seen before was called up to the stage. His name was Jag. She'd passed him on her way up the aisle.

She'd noticed him even before that because he looked like such an oddball. He was tall and thin, with dark skin and black hair—she thought he might be Indian— but that's not what was odd about him. He had ramrod-straight posture and an oddly blank expression. He was wear-ing a kid-sized suit and tie and shiny black leather shoes. He'd been sitting alone, like Kate, not talking to anybody else.

She had to admit he had con-fidence, though. Jag waved off Mr. Lee's offer to accompany him on the piano because he'd brought with him—could it really be?—a ukulele, which he was going to play while he sang.

The ukulele looked like something you would buy in a toy shop. It had a picture on it of a man who was wearing a bright yellow Hawaiian shirt, and the man was himself playing a ukulele. Kate couldn't see whether there was a smaller man on that man's ukulele who was also playing the ukulele, with an even smaller man on that one. But she wouldn't have been at all surprised.

The song that Jag played was...weird. His voice was high, and the melody was meandering and sort of spooky—it was barely a melody at all, it just sort of wandered around. The lyrics were something about a magic boy who goes on some kind of a journey? And then learns something about love? All accompanied by the plaintive twanging of the ukulele.

At the end Jag bowed. There were some snickers from the hall, and somebody did a falsetto impression of Jag's singing until Mr. Lee glared out at the audience. All in all, Kate was just glad that somebody had humiliated himself even more comprehensively than she had at the auditions.

But then—*but then*—when the cast list went up on Thursday, guess whose name was right up there at the top, next to that of Billy Crocker, the brash young stowaway who gets to sing "It's De-Lovely" with beguiling young heiress Hope Harcourt?

Jag's Name, That's Whose

BUT KATE PUT THAT OUT OF HER MIND AS THE *SILVER Arrow* chuffed its way through the forest behind her house. Whatever. Stupid musical. She had way more important things to do.

"Where are we even going?" said Tom.

DON'T ASK ME

I'M ONLY THE TRAIN, THAT'S ALL

JUST A GIANT POWERFUL MAGIC STEAM TRAIN

ASK "THE CONDUCTOR"

"We're going to the Rail Yard," Kate said. "For all of your information."

Tom sat slumped on his stool, radiating a lack of enthusiasm. He'd decided that that stool was his, the one on the right, so he'd written *TOM* on a piece of masking tape in Magic Marker and stuck it onto the seat.

"Why there?"

"Because we always go to the Rail Yard."

That was true. They couldn't fit a whole train on the tracks behind their house, just the engine, so whenever they finished a mission they dropped off the extra cars at the Rail Yard before they went home.

"We don't need a whole train just to look for Uncle Herbert."

"We're not going there to get a train," Kate said. "We're going to talk to the dispatcher."

"Why would the dispatcher know where Uncle Herbert is?"

"Well, it's worth a try."

"This is a stupid plan."

"*You're* a stupid plan!"

It wasn't a very good comeback.

They felt their stomachs drop as the *Silver Arrow* reached the hill in the woods behind their house and plunged down it. They spent the next few minutes in matching irritable silences. Tom's was presumably because he was wishing he was somewhere else. Kate's was because Tom was right—it wasn't a very good plan—but she didn't know what else to do, and she had to do something.

She didn't have to dwell on it for very long, because a couple of minutes later they almost died.

Kate knew there were other trains out there riding the rails of the Great Secret Intercontinental Railway. She saw them once in a while, though only ever from far away, cruising along distant parallel tracks or waiting at a station while the *Silver Arrow* blew by them at full steam. She was curious about them, but she never had a chance to stop and meet the people who drove them. It wasn't like there was a clubhouse or a social night or something where the conductors all got together.

At night the train lights looked cozy and inviting

in the distance. She supposed the *Silver Arrow*'s lights must look cozy and inviting to them, too.

But now Kate saw something distinctly uninviting. She didn't notice it at first, till the *Silver Arrow* started saying:

BLAZE

BLAZE

BLAZING

BLAZER

"What?" Tom said. "Use actual words!"

But apparently the *Silver Arrow* couldn't even speak because it just printed:

```
       ^
     / | \
   /   |   \
       |
       |
       |
       |
```

Kate slung her head out the window. Dead ahead was a flash of sunlight off metal. Above it hung a puff of steam. There was another train on the same track they were on, a couple of miles away but closing fast. Too fast. Steam trains don't stop on a dime.

"Those lunatics," she whispered. "What are they doing?"

WE'RE THE ONES WITHOUT A TIMETABLE

WE'RE THE LUNATICS!

Tom went for the brake lever, but Kate put a hand on it.

"No. Full speed."

"What?!" Tom shouted. "You're going to kill us! Even faster than we would've died anyway!"

"Just trust me! Shovel! More steam!"

It felt wrong to her too, but sometimes you have to listen to your feelings and other times you have to push them away and do the exact opposite. Like when she'd had that feeling that she should audition for *Anything Goes*. Should've done the opposite! The trick was knowing when to do which one.

To his credit Tom did what she said: He grabbed a shovel from its hook on the wall and started slamming coal into the firebox while she pushed the throttle as high as it went. The landscape whipped by faster and faster, and the rhythm of the *Silver Arrow*'s puffing and the *clickety-clack*ing of the track merged into one long, rising rattle.

Kate's brain was speeding up, too. She'd seen old-timey pictures of what happened when two steam trains smashed into each other head-first. In fact, since she became a conductor she'd become quite an amateur historian of gruesome railway disasters. This one time—it was in 1896, in Texas—a bunch of people had taken two locomotives and deliberately smashed them into each other head-on at full speed and charged admission for people to come and watch, because apparently people did stupid things just for fun even before the internet. When the trains hit, both boilers exploded, and the blast was so big two people in the audience were killed.

Kate locked in the throttle and reverser and grabbed the other shovel off the wall. She opened the window of the train and hung way out to one side as far as she could. She could see the other train clearly now. The drivers were probably panicking as badly as she was. They weren't even blowing their whistle—there was no point. No way could they slow down in time.

"Kate!" Tom was terrified. "We're going to hit it!"

"No, we're not!"

"We have to jump!"

"Don't jump!"

Fifty yards ahead of them the track forked. Leaning out as far as she could and swinging the shovel with one hand like a sword, Kate whacked the switching lever.

Her whole arm went numb, and the shovel went spinning off who knows where—the force of the impact tore it right out of her hand. But she must have hit the switch hard enough, because when the *Silver Arrow* slammed into the junction it swung hard to the left onto the branch line, so hard it felt like the force was going to throw her out the window, or the train would derail, or both.

But they didn't. A split second later the other train boomed past them with an almighty roar and a blast of wind, close enough that she could swear it touched her hair. Then the *Silver Arrow* was off and rattling safely down the branch line.

Kate hauled herself back into the cab and collapsed on its grubby metal floor, weak with relief. She

rubbed her numb arm. Tom was sitting on his stool hugging himself, breathing fast.

"That was too close," he said.

REALLY? YOU THINK SO?

BECAUSE I THOUGHT MAYBE WE COULD CUT IT A LITTLE CLOSER NEXT TIME

"I'm sorry I said you were a stupid plan," Kate whispered. "I'm glad those weren't my last words."

"Thank you."

DO YOU UNDERSTAND NOW WHY YOU DON'T TAKE TRIPS WITHOUT A TIMETABLE?

"Yes," Kate snapped. "Give me a little credit."

ALSO YOU LOST MY SHOVEL

"I'm sorry I lost your shovel."

CAN WE GO BACK NOW PLEASE?

"No."

This was her idea, it was on her, and she'd already almost gotten them all killed. But they would never get another timetable without Herbert, and if they didn't get another timetable, how many animals would die? How many quokkas would be burned up? (A quokka looks like a kangaroo that went through the dryer by mistake and shrunk. They're supercute and only exist on about three islands off the coast of Australia.) She didn't know if what she was doing was right or wrong, but frankly she felt like she'd been getting a lot of things wrong lately, and she was desperate to do something right for a change—to fix some problem, anything really. The image of that speeding train kept playing in Kate's head like a video loop, except every time it had a different ending where they didn't make it to the junction in time.

Kate had gotten an unpleasantly close look at the train as it roared by. It was painted a golden yellow and built in a very different style, all streamlined curves and chrome highlights and sleek lines. Not at all like the chunky black utilitarian design of the *Silver Arrow*. If it were possible for a steam train to look futuristic, then that's how that other train looked.

On the side of its tender was written a name:

The Golden Swift

The Most Dangerous
Bird in the World

IT WAS ALWAYS NIGHT AT THE RAIL YARD AND ALWAYS
snowing. Kate had been there many times now, but

the experience of going to cold, wintry darkness straight from a sunny Sunday morning still made her a little dizzy. It was not unlike that weightless drop going down the steep hill in the woods. Even Tom looked around solemnly at the magic of it all.

The Rail Yard was an enormous clearing surrounded by woods and covered with a squiggling mess of steel rails on which stood the Great Secret Intercontinental Railway's vast collection of train cars: wooden boxcars, rusting tankers, hoppers, flat cars, luxurious old-fashioned sleepers, dining cars, precious little red cabooses and some even more exotic and mysterious ones. Sometimes Kate liked to just wander among them, reading the random

numbers on their sides, wondering what was in them and where they'd been.

But today wasn't a wandering day. Right in the middle of that great nest of metal spaghetti was a small lighted shack that belonged—or so Uncle Herbert had always told her—to someone known as the dispatcher, who was in charge of all those cars. Kate had never seen this individual. Whoever they were, they hid away in their shack, a bit like the Once-ler in *The Lorax*.

But tonight Kate was going to meet the dispatcher. Doing her best to shake off her brush with death, she picked her way across the frozen wooden railroad ties, thick oak slabs that smelled of creosote. Kate always winced inwardly to think of all the trees that must have been cut down to make them. Maybe they only used fallen timber. Or maybe it was magic. She hoped so. After all, she had once—for a year, or maybe just a dreaming hour—been a tree herself.

"Thank you for coming with me," Kate said.

Tom shrugged. "Sure."

"I know you have other stuff to do."

"Yeah."

Kate stood up very straight, took a shaky breath, and knocked on the wooden door of the shack. The door was old, with peeling white paint, and didn't fit very neatly in its frame. Kate knew she wasn't supposed to be out here. She was violating the chain of command. Also she was shivering from the cold. She always forgot to dress for the chill of the Rail Yard.

The door swung open, and standing there in the lighted doorway was the closest thing to a velociraptor that Kate had ever seen in real life. It was an enormous bird, taller than she was, something like an ostrich but with a blue head, black feathers, and two huge, scaly gray feet.

She hadn't known what to expect, but this wasn't even on her bingo card.

"Can I help you?"

"Hi. Uh." She found her voice. "I was looking for the dispatcher?"

"You found her. If you're wondering I'm a cassowary, the most dangerous bird in the world."

The bird's manner was smooth and sophisticated. Almost—and Kate did not use this word lightly—*debonair.* You noticed it more because the cassowary's appearance was so absurd. In addition to her blue head she had a bright red wattle and a huge bony crest that looked like an oversized helmet. It was bigger than the rest of her actual head. She wore a little key on a string around her neck.

Behind her was a cramped but tidy office. Kate couldn't help but eye the bird's feet, which were so big that they seemed like they should belong to some even larger and more reptilian creature. There were three toes on each one, and the innermost toe on each foot had a dagger-like claw five inches long.

"We're looking for our uncle," Tom said. "Uncle Herbert."

"I take it you mean Junior Field Agent Herbert Yastremzski."

"That is...who we mean. I think." Kate had never

thought of Uncle Herbert as a junior anything, but well, there it was. Junior Field Agent Yastremzski. She would never look at him the same way again.

"He's eight weeks and five days late with his latest assignment." The cassowary had a very serious way of talking, as if she were a superspy telling Kate the secret password to disable the nuclear device that was going to explode in ten seconds and kill them all. "In that time we've defaulted on approximately two hundred and eighty-seven calamity-class rescues, removals, and relocations."

"That sounds bad," Kate said.

"It is. Very. I assume you two are his replacements."

"We're just his niece and nephew. We're conductors."

The cassowary put her thick, horny bill right up in their faces.

"Humans. An invasive species. And juvenile specimens, if I'm not mistaken."

"We're not 'specimens.'" Figuring it was now or never, put up or shut up, Kate drew herself up and activated the voice she used when addressing disobedient train passengers. "We may be juvenile—and invasive, I guess—but we are also official conductors of the Great Secret Intercontinental Railway, and we're here on the *Silver Arrow* to get our uncle back."

"Are you. And what are your current theories regarding your uncle's disappearance?"

"We don't have any."

"May I see your timetable?"

"You may not," Tom said, "because we don't have one of those, either."

"I see." The great bird's milky nictitating membranes flicked sidewise across her eyes, an unnerving sight. "In other words, you have—I believe the expression is—'gone rogue.'"

"That," Kate said, "is exactly what we've gone."

Kate shivered and hugged herself, but she willed herself not to drop the cassowary's gaze. The bird tapped one of her long talons on the floor in thought.

"I like it," the dispatcher said finally. "I take it you're going to want some train cars?"

The Premium Rolling Slumberliner

"THIS IS *SO GREAT*," KATE SAID, NOT FOR THE FIRST TIME. "This is the greatest thing in the history of great things."

"Beats how Junior Agent Yastremzski used to do it, anyway," Tom said.

The first time they'd come to the Rail Yard, Uncle Herbert had put them through a whole rigmarole about how they had to come up with their own ideas for train cars. They'd sat there feeling vaguely foolish trying to think of something, anything, and he'd lorded it over them deciding which cars they could or could not have. Only after he'd done that did he relay their requests to the dispatcher.

But now they'd cut out the middleman and were dealing directly with the dispatcher herself, and that was a whole different story. After their initial interrogation, the cassowary ushered them into her office and simply handed over a fat, neatly handwritten logbook that listed every piece of rolling stock in the yard. All they had to do was pick from the list, exactly like ordering off a menu. (Which was exactly what Uncle Herbert had always said it was *not* like.)

It was anybody's guess who did all that neat handwriting, since the cassowary didn't have hands, but Kate let that one lie. It was just such a relief that something on this mission was going well! She didn't want to be greedy, so she started with the usual useful stuff: passenger cars, dining cars, flats, boxes, caboose. The tools of the trade. Then she got down to business.

"Sauna car?" Kate said, flipping through the binder.

"Too hot."

"That's literally the point of a sauna car. To be hot."

"You don't even like saunas," Tom said. "That one time we stayed in that hotel when Dad took us to the fishing museum, you lasted like thirty seconds in the sauna before you ran out of there."

"True." Kate pursed her lips thoughtfully. "Kaleidoscope car...ballroom car...crystal car... exploding car? How would that work?"

"There's a bank car. Think it comes with money in it? There should just be a money car."

"Transparent car, jungle-gym car, paper car,

aquarium car, spinning car…grapefruit car? Upside-down car? Some of these don't even make sense."

"Trampoline car!" Tom said. "Let's get that!"

"Jumping on a trampoline in a moving train car? Does that really sound like a good idea? Look, there's a mirror car."

"And a dojo car."

"Uncle Herbert said no weapons, though."

"Uncle Herbert's not here," Tom said. "And it doesn't matter anyway, because—"

"—because your body is the weapon?"

"My body is the weapon."

It was something they said a lot in hapkido.

Kate read through the binders for longer than was probably strictly compatible with the fact that they were supposed to be on an urgent quest right now. In the end she asked the dispatcher for a garden car, a dojo car (you're welcome), and an observatory car. And an invisible car, for no reason whatsoever, and another library car, and another candy car, plus an ice cream car, too, on the principle that too much is never enough. Kate also noticed that there were quite a variety of sleeper cars available, in addition to the standard ones they'd gotten in the past, and she decided they were ready for an upgrade. She settled on something called the Premium Rolling Slumberliner. The name alone made Kate feel pleasantly drowsy.

Or maybe it wasn't just the name. You lost track of time on these magic journeys—it was midafternoon when they left home and her body clock was telling her it was time for bed. The dispatcher had disappeared into a back room with their list. Kate followed to ask her how long she thought they'd have to wait.

She was glad she did because laid out on a huge table in that back room was the biggest, most magnificent train set you could possibly imagine. It was a fantastically detailed model of the Rail Yard outside, with each curve and loop of track, each tie, each car, each switch, each tiny glowing light reproduced with absolute precision. The cars were miniature marvels, each one maybe two inches long, with perfect little wheels and markings like the gears in a watch. There was even a tiny model *Silver Arrow.*

Along one side of the table was a long panel of knobs and switches, and the cassowary was poking away at them with surprising delicacy. As she did, one tiny car after another sprang to life and moved of its own accord along the intricate system of tracks to its place behind the little *Silver Arrow*, where it coupled itself on.

Tom came in behind her. He gasped and crouched down so his eyes were level with the table and peered into the cab of the tiny *Silver Arrow*.

"It's perfect. It's even got tiny shovels." He squinted. "It's even got the teeny-tiny piece of tape on the stool where I wrote my name."

Kate watched the model cars swing around the curves of track and link up with the *Silver Arrow*. She also watched Tom. It had been a while since she'd heard that note of wonder in his voice. *See?* she thought. *Pretty cool, isn't it?*

But she didn't say anything. When someone's feeling that good, why rub their nose in it?

Once the cassowary had finished her work Kate said good night, and she and Tom stepped out of the warm shed into the cold darkness. The snow was falling thicker now, tiny, dusty flakes. The world looked black and white in the harsh illumination of the over-head lights.

A brand-new train stood behind the *Silver Arrow*, dark and gleaming, but she didn't have the energy to explore it right now. Instead she and Tom just walked along it, trailing their fingers against the cold metal, till they came to the twin Slumberliners, identical except for their names over the doors.

They were both a deep midnight blue and longer by half than their usual sleepers. Kate waved good night to Tom and climbed the steps. The doors opened by themselves.

The lights came on by themselves, too, softly. Inside was something closer to a tiny house than just a sleeper car. There was a fireplace with a fire already softly crackling in it. There was a fridge full of midnight snacks, and a wardrobe hung with conductor's uniforms, and a shelf of books. The bathroom wasn't cramped like a regular train bathroom; it had a proper tub you could stretch out in. It was nicer than their bathroom at home.

Likewise the bed itself wasn't just a bunk but a proper bed that filled almost the full width of the car, covered with a deep, thick comforter like a layer of whipped cream, and a pair of soft marshmallow pillows, and silk pajamas laid out on top of all that.

Kate slipped into the pajamas, slipped herself under the covers, and slept.

The Fastest Bird
in the World

THE NEXT MORNING KATE AND TOM WERE UP FRONT IN the cab of the *Silver Arrow*, feeling well rested and well fed and just generally *well*.

Kate slung her arm out the window. They were steaming through a dense forest of smooth-barked gray trees with wiggly branches. It had been two months since Kate last rode in the *Silver Arrow*, and she'd forgotten how good it felt. She knew who she was here. In school it felt like everybody was always telling you who you were, and it was never who you wanted to be—it was like the play: They were always casting you, and you were never Hope Harcourt.

You were only ever in the chorus. But not here. Why couldn't she feel like this in school?

She almost jumped when a small, fierce blue head on the end of a long slender neck poked into the cab. She hadn't realized the cassowary was on board.

"Are you sure you should be here?" Tom said. "I mean, with a couple of rogue operators like us? What if the Board of Directors finds out?"

"Where you're going you may need backup."

"Who's going to do the dispatching while you're gone?"

"The backup dispatcher." The cassowary didn't

miss a beat. "A good dispatcher always has backup. Take this."

Standing on one leg, the cassowary offered Kate a slip of paper impaled on one of her disturbingly long talons. She took it.

"This is Uncle Herbert's address," Kate said.

"That's correct."

"I went there already. He's not there. Did you run a public records search, too?"

"The dispatcher of the Great Secret Intercontinental Railway doesn't need public records," the enormous bird said. "I have private records."

With that she withdrew her bony crested head and disappeared.

"Do you think it's really true," Tom said, "about her being the world's most dangerous bird?"

"There's a lot of birds in the world. I guess one of them must be the most dangerous."

"I always thought it would be an eagle, though. Or a hawk. Not like an ostrich that got colored in wrong."

I THINK WE SHOULD GO TO THE ADDRESS

"He's not there!" Kate said again.

MAYBE YOU MISSED SOMETHING

"I'm pretty sure I— Wait. Is this one of those times when you know something I don't, but you're not just coming out and saying it?"

YES

"I hate those times."

THEY'RE MY FAVORITE TIMES

Twenty minutes later the *Silver Arrow* came to a stop in what looked to Kate like an empty field in the middle of nowhere. The cassowary got out and unlocked a special switch lever with the little key around her neck. Kate couldn't see any branch line for them to switch onto, but the *Silver Arrow* rolled forward anyway, and just when it looked like they were about to plunge off the track...they didn't plunge.

There was a branch line. It was just invisible.

I'VE HEARD ABOUT THESE

BUT THEY'VE NEVER LET ME GO ON ONE BEFORE!

"You're welcome," Kate said.

The invisible branch line wound up and up into the air in a wide ascending spiral, higher and higher. Not as high as when they'd used the rocket car, but high enough that the wind whipped up and gusts of it pushed at the train and Kate pulled her arm back inside. The cassowary came back and stood at the window, watching a flock of small birds. They were amazingly athletic fliers, swooping and diving and turning on a dime.

"What are they?" Kate said.

"Swifts."

"Another invasive species?"

Kate had had quite an earful from her animal friends about invasive species and how they were all humans' fault. Not that it wasn't completely true. But she felt like her ears were just about full up at the moment, with all the bushfires and global warming and the rest of the bad news.

"Not at all," the cassowary said. "I just like to watch them. Did you know swifts are the fastest fliers in the world?"

"Wrong," said Tom. "Peregrine falcon."

He always knew that kind of thing: biggest, fastest, strongest, heaviest, etc.

"Only when they're diving for prey," the cassowary said. "If you had a race from point A to point B, the swifts would win every time. And they're long-distance fliers, too. They weigh about as much as a mouse, but some of them migrate to Peru and back every year. Swifts spend almost their whole lives flying—they barely ever land. They eat and sleep and mate in the air."

Her voice sounded a little dreamy. The cassowary's own wings were almost comically tiny and vestigial. She probably would've liked wings that worked, Kate thought. I mean, Kate would've liked wings, and she wasn't even a bird.

"They don't look very dangerous." Kate thought that might make the cassowary feel better.

"No. Not so dangerous."

By now they were rolling smoothly through the air high above the city of Chicago, approaching the cluster of skyscrapers that made up downtown. Soon Kate could pick out that impossibly slim, expensive-looking tower that just the other day she and her wet, out-of-sorts mom had stood in front of. She didn't

think she'd want to live there—it was so tall and thin it looked like the wind would break it in half at any moment. As the train rolled closer, three extra stories flickered into existence on top of it. They sort of bent into view, as if some trick of the light had been concealing them till you looked at just the right angle.

Kate had never given much thought to what her uncle Herbert's home might look like—to say she lacked curiosity about her uncle's personal life would have been an understatement—but she realized now that if she *had* thought about it, she would've underestimated how awesome it was. He lived in a secret invisible triplex apartment at the top of a deluxe skyscraper.

"I am," Tom said, "grudgingly impressed."

Herbert's apartment even had its own personal train station: The invisible tracks went in through an archway and pulled up at a neat little platform. It was like having your own private elevator, except way better.

They got out. There were no railings on the edge of the platform, and Kate and Tom huddled together for moral support. No one answered when they knocked on the door, so Kate pushed on it lightly, and it swung open.

She and Tom looked at each other.

"I guess you wouldn't worry about burglars up here," Tom said softly.

"I guess."

Cautiously they stepped inside.

"Or maybe you would."

Immediately Kate envied Uncle Herbert's apartment a lot less, because the entire place had been torn to pieces.

A Spot of Bother

KATE REACHED FOR TOM'S HAND. IT HAD BEEN A COUPLE of years since she'd done that, but when she saw Herbert's apartment she did it instinctively.

The place wasn't just a mess, like Herbert had forgotten to pick up his socks or something. Everything was on the floor: books, lamps, bowls, plates. There were the splintered remains of a cello, a toppled grandfather clock, a shattered old chandelier, and what looked like a whole collection of smashed ships-in-bottles. Pillows and cushions had been torn open, and their stuffing was scattered everywhere.

Pictures were pulled out of their frames. Everything that could be broken was broken.

This was not typical Herbert. Problems involving Uncle Herbert generally ended up being humorous misunderstandings or something of that ilk. This was a different kind of trouble. Not kid trouble. Grown-up trouble.

"It looks," the cassowary said coolly, "as though Junior Agent Yastremzski has had a spot of bother."

"I'll say." Kate swallowed nervously.

"They must've been searching for something," Tom said.

"Like what? What could Uncle Herbert have that anybody could possibly want?" Kate called out: "Uncle Herbert?"

Silence.

"The Great Secret Intercontinental Railway does have its enemies," the cassowary said ominously.

"We do?" Tom said. "Cool."

"Who would be against the GSIR?" Kate knew some people didn't believe in climate change, but it was hard to argue with saving animals. Wasn't it?

"There's nothing so reasonable and good that somebody somewhere won't figure out a way to be against it."

Kate started picking her way through the mess.

"You'd think the railway would take a little more interest in retrieving its kidnapped employees," she said, "instead of just leaving it up to us conductors."

"The railway's resources are limited," the cassowary said, "and its faith in its conductors is unlimited."

That was flattering, but not very helpful. Where's the Great Secret Intercontinental Police Department when you need it?

Kate wandered through the rooms, which

contained a lot of furniture made out of shiny metal rods. *This must be what they call a "bachelor pad,"* she thought. She tried not to be critical of what was left of the interior decoration. She didn't want to think ill of the maybe-possibly dead. There was a giant living room on the second floor with a correspondingly giant TV, now lying facedown amid the shards of a smashed glass coffee table. Tom looked almost as sad about the TV as he did about Uncle Herbert.

Kate just hoped they found him soon because the tension was getting to be a bit much. She picked up a pillow and tried to study it like a police officer would. It didn't look like someone had cut it with scissors or a knife. It looked like it had been ripped apart.

"I don't think a person could do this," she said. "It looks more like an animal."

"Get out of my house."

She jumped. The voice was low and growly and snarly and definitely not Uncle Herbert's.

A creature that Kate didn't recognize was watching them from the staircase leading to the top floor. He had huge fangs and thick wiry fur, and his dark eyes burned with hatred. He was about the size of a dog, but a dog that had been crossbred with a bear and then  maybe possessed by a demon.

Tom got over his shock first.

"Hi! We're looking for our uncle Herbert."

"No uncles here. This is my house, you tree-killing chimpanzees. Get out."

"This is not your house," Kate said, more bravely than she felt. "This is Uncle Herbert's house. What are you doing here?"

"None of your business!"

Kate was just wondering what she would do if the demon-dog came any closer when the cassowary arrived.

"Oh dear," the big bird said. "We're going to need a better answer than that."

She didn't wait for a reply but walked deliberately toward the stairs where the creature was crouching.

The cassowary's legs bent backward like the heron's, but they weren't thin reeds like the heron's were.

"No? Suit yourself."

The animal bared his teeth, which were absolutely enormous. They looked like vampire teeth you'd buy at a joke shop. The cassowary began climbing the stairs.

This ought to be good, Kate thought.

The demon-dog gathered himself, snarled, and leaped. Time slowed down. If it were Kate, she would've curled up into a ball, but the cassowary didn't hesitate or flinch. Instead she sprang smoothly into the air to meet her attacker and with a single powerful pump of her massive thigh kicked him full in the chest.

It was like he'd hit a wall: He reversed course in midair and flew backward up the stairs. The cassowary climbed after him. At the top the demon-dog recovered himself and turned and hissed, but the cassowary just kicked him again, and he went tumbling and sliding backward on the hardwood floor.

By the time Kate caught up to them the cassowary was standing on top of him, pinning him. He

looked stunned. When he tried to move, the cassowary bent down and pecked him on the top of his head.

She really was pretty dangerous, Kate thought. And she hadn't even used her claws.

"Now," the cassowary said, gazing down calmly at her prisoner. "Explain your presence here."

"Why don't you explain your stupid blue head!"

The cassowary pecked him again.

"All right," Kate said, "I think you can get off the—sorry, what exactly are you?"

"What are *you*?" the animal shot back.

"I'm a human," Kate said. "My name is Kate. That's Tom."

"Also human," Tom said.

"And the bird that's standing on you is a cassowary."

"World's most dangerous bird," said the cassowary.

"I really think you can get off him now."

She did. The animal got up on all fours, shook himself angrily, and glared at them.

"I'm a wolverine, you ignorant bipeds. Now get out of my house."

Kate was really glad she hadn't known the wolverine was a wolverine before the cassowary got in a fight with him. She was a lot more familiar with superheroes named after wolverines than she was with actual wolverines, but what little she knew based on that was enough to make her pretty cautious.

"What did you do with Uncle Herbert?"

"I ate him."

Kate froze.

"Nonsense," the cassowary said. "Wolverines are not man-eaters."

"Yes, we are!"

"No. You aren't."

"How confident would you say you are about that?" Kate asked the cassowary quietly, eyeing the wolverine's teeth. "I mean, on a scale of one to ten?"

"Wild dogs will eat humans," the bird said with authority. "Wolves, bears, and big cats will. But not a wolverine. They may look scary, but wolverines are members of the mustelid family. In other words this animal is just a very large weasel."

Everybody looked at the wolverine. His eyes blazed with a dark, unquenchable fury.

"I hate you," he said.

Detective Kate

"I'M GOING TO ASK YOU AGAIN," KATE SAID. "IF YOU didn't eat Uncle Herbert—which I'm almost totally one hundred percent sure you didn't—then what are you doing in his house?"

"This is my house."

"No, it isn't!"

It took a long time to get the story out of him. The wolverine was what they referred to in TV shows about lawyers as an "uncooperative witness." As far as they could tell, he was from somewhere in northern Canada, but he'd been having trouble there with hunters who were after his fur. Also lately there had been less and less snow around, and wolverines need snow—the females use it to make the dens where they raise little wolverines. He was fed up with it.

That was when he found a train ticket, tucked inside a deer carcass. The problem was, he didn't want it.

"You didn't *want* it?" Tom asked.

"You really think I would get on a train driven by human beings?" the wolverine spat. "Humans hunt us! Humans are heating up the planet! And now you say you're going to save us? Leave us alone!"

"We're just trying to help!"

"Well, stop it!"

Kate didn't know what to say to that. She hadn't known there were animals who felt that way. But of course there were. Why would they trust humans? Maybe the wolverine was one of those enemies the cassowary was talking about.

The wolverine hadn't wanted the train ticket, but he couldn't stay where he was, either. So once the train was gone, he set off along the tracks.

"Humans made those tracks," Tom pointed out.

"Are you sure? How do you know?"

"Well…who else?"

The wolverine snorted. It was true that they still didn't know who'd built the Great Secret Intercontinental Railway, or who ran it, or really much of anything about it. If Kate ever tracked down that Board of Directors, she would have a few questions for them.

But first she had to track down Uncle Herbert.

Wolverines can walk enormous distances, and this one had walked along the tracks till he was exhausted and almost dead from hunger and thirst. The station he finally got to, after all that walking, was Uncle Herbert's apartment.

"Was it already like this? All messed up?"

"No," the wolverine admitted.

"Okay. Well, good job. You ate Herbert's house."

Even if wolverines won't eat humans, they'll eat almost anything else, and having consumed every-thing edible and semi-edible in the apartment, the wolverine had again been on the verge of starvation when Kate and Tom and the cassowary turned up.

He really didn't seem to know anything at all about Uncle Herbert.

"I've got some challenging news for you," Kate said. "We've got a train outside with a whole dining car full of food. So you can have some food that has human cooties on it, or you can stay here and starve to death. Your choice."

"Starve," the wolverine hissed.

Kate sighed and went off to search for clues.

She wandered aimlessly through the rooms of the triple-decker apartment. It had incredible views, but she wasn't in a mood to admire them. She supposed it was exciting that on top of being a conductor she now got to be a detective, too. Who hasn't wanted to be a detective? She crunched through broken coffee cups and torn yellow Herbert-suits and a tube of tooth-paste that the wolverine had apparently squashed all the toothpaste out of and then lapped it up.

But the thing you never thought about when you

thought about being a detective was the vast majority of things in the world that *aren't* clues. There were a lot of those to sift through.

Meanwhile the fact that there were so many animals out there who were starving or being hunted or running from bushfires was kind of building up in Kate's mind like air in a balloon, and she felt like if she didn't find a way to do something about it soon, her head was going to pop. But she couldn't give up. You had to be like a swift: You just kept flying, eating and sleeping on the wing, never landing till you got there.

On the top floor of Herbert's apartment there was a room full of gym equipment, obviously never used; a wine closet, heavily used; a hot tub in which the wolverine had done something unspeakable; and a small room with an old-fashioned desk that was so solidly built that even the wolverine hadn't been able to destroy it, though he'd pulled out all the drawers and thoroughly gnawed the corners.

Papers were scattered everywhere. Quite a lot of them were blank timetables, without the times and destinations filled in. Kate stirred them aimlessly with her foot.

Then she noticed one that wasn't completely blank. It had something hastily scribbled on it, in Herbert's handwriting. She picked it up.

The word written on the timetable was *ACHNASHELLACH*.

Nasal Lace

"I'M NOT EVEN COMPLETELY SURE THAT *IS* A WORD," TOM
said.

They were back in the cab of the *Silver Arrow*,
which had been waiting patiently this whole time on
the tracks outside Herbert's apartment. It was still
late spring, and it was chilly in the shade of the private station. The *Arrow*'s boiler ticked as it cooled.

"Of course it's a word," Kate said, a little defen-
sively. "It's *the* word! It's a clue!"

"Then what does it mean?"

"I don't know! Maybe it's a name! Like the name
of the kidnapper, which Herbert scribbled down

at the last minute, right before they broke the door down! Or maybe it's the reason *why* Herbert was kidnapped, or whatever happened to him! *They* didn't want us to know about Atch-na-shell-atch"—it was kind of a mouthful to say—"but now"—she finished dramatically—"we do!"

Tom spun lazily around on TOM's stool.

"So where does that leave us?"

Kate spun on her stool, too, slowly, on the off chance it would give her an inspiration. For a minute the two of them just sat there, rotating.

"Maybe we're supposed to rearrange the letters," Tom said. "Like a nanogram."

"Anagram. But yeah, maybe we are!"

They sat in silence for another minute, trying to rearrange the letters in their heads to spell something. Kate wished she had a Scrabble set. They should've asked for a board games car.

"I got *HALLE CHA-CHAS*," Tom said finally. "But there's an *N* left over."

"You did better than me. All I got was *NASAL LACE*."

YOU MIGHT BE INTERESTED TO KNOW

THAT ACHNASHELLACH IS THE NAME OF A
FOREST IN SCOTLAND

"What? It is?" Kate felt a small flutter of hope in her chest. "Is it a special forest? Like secret or magic or something?"

NO

IT'S JUST A BUNCH OF TREES STANDING NEXT
TO EACH OTHER

"But still! Why didn't you say anything?"

BECAUSE YOU'RE GOING TO MAKE US GO THERE

"You're darn right I am!"

IT'S A LONG WAY FROM CHICAGO

"Then we'd better get started." Kate was already at the controls, checking the water gauge, raising the pressure. "The game is afoot!"

NO IT ISN'T

"You're just bitter because you don't have feet." Finally, finally, she was starting to get somewhere.

I'm coming, Uncle Herbert! she thought. *Hold on!* And once she had Herbert back, everything would go back to normal.

"Do I have to come?" Tom said.

"Yes!"

"Why?"

"Because conductors need backup. Come on, we can check out the ice cream car on the way."

★

But they didn't make it all the way to the ice cream car because they had to go through the dojo car first and Tom got distracted. It was a lovely little car with wood paneling, big sunny windows, mats on the floor, and a couple of heavy punching bags hanging from chains. There were also rows of weapons along the walls: nunchucks, staffs, swords, and other stuff she didn't know the names of.

She left Tom there practicing with his nunchucks and walked farther back, stopping along the way to collect a handful of Maltesers from the candy car. She was impatient to get to Achnashellach, and she shoved more of them into her mouth at once than she probably would have done if anybody had been watching. They were crossing a stretch of ocean, and colossal swells were booming along beside them, almost keeping pace with the train, their peaks breaking out in crests of white foam.

The next car in line was the garden car. It was basically a greenhouse on wheels, neatly constructed out of hundreds of panes of glass held together by an intricate tracery of wrought iron. Inside was an absolute riot of plant life.

Kate was an animals person, and she knew about as little about plants as it was possible for a carbon-based life-form on the planet Earth to know. But she knew what she liked, and she liked the look of the garden car, which was stuffed with ferns and climbing vines, shrubs and bushes, big blousy blossoms and little chains of neat stars and everything in between. Swallowing the last of the Maltesers, she opened the delicate glass door and went in.

A thick smell embraced her, many-layered like a cake, of pollen and rich earth and humid air. For a second it was so lovely and relaxing that she closed her eyes and just bathed in it.

Then every alarm bell in Kate's brain went off at once.

Her palms started to sweat. Her breath caught and her pulse raced and her stomach tightened. Something was jangling every nerve in her body. It was a sound, and the sound was buzzing. The buzzing of *bees*.

Kate had had a bad experience once. When she was six, she and a couple of friends had been exploring some fields near her house, looking for a secret hideout. They'd found a good one—a big, thick bush with enough space underneath that you could crawl inside it.

But they hadn't been there long when Kate heard a strange wailing sound. One of her friends was crying and frantically waving her arms around. At first Kate just stared at her, not even alarmed—she couldn't figure out what the problem was. Then she noticed little black shapes whirling around her. Then they were whirling around Kate, too, in an angry storm, bouncing off her. Dots of pain were blooming all over her.

They ran for it. They didn't even say anything, just bolted for their different houses. Among Kate's good qualities as a six-year-old was not stoicism, and she cried hysterically the whole way home. Horribly, the swarm *followed* them, chasing them all the way, and a few even infiltrated their way into Kate's house and had to be hunted down and squashed by her fearless mom.

In retrospect the whole incident was hardly life threatening, but it was really painful and somehow so permanently terrifying that to this day Kate was extremely unheroic in the presence of any swarming, buzzing, stinging insects.

And yes, she knew about bees. They were good for the planet. They pollinated things. They usually minded their own business. They could not actually smell your fear. And, okay, in actual fact the swarm she'd gotten into trouble with had turned out to be yellowjackets, which weren't bees at all, they were wasps. Though they looked a lot like bees.

Still. Just the sound was enough to freeze her with panic right there in the doorway of the greenhouse car. The hum grew louder, and as it did, it shaped itself into words.

"I am bees!" it said. *"I am bees! I am bees!"*

No. No way. She ran, slamming the glass door of the greenhouse car behind her. She was all for saving nature. But some nature she just didn't want to be stuck in a train car with.

Achnashellach

IT WAS TWILIGHT IN SCOTLAND.

The landscape was different from any that Kate had ever seen before, humpy and green and threadbare—it looked like a thin carpet of grass had been laid down and then someone had tried to hide a lot of boulders under it, but not very well, so that rocky shapes poked up through it in places.

Achnashellach itself was a patchy forest of scrappy pine trees, very rough and very remote—the kind of place you could get lost in as soon as you stepped ten feet off the path. They *clickety-clack*ed through the twilight wilderness, Tom and Kate and the cassowary all together in the cab of the *Silver Arrow*. Kate was grateful for the train's huge, hot, comforting presence, and Tom's, and even the cassowary's— basically she was grateful for anyone who wasn't a stinging insect right now.

If possible she would drop the garden car off back at the Rail Yard at the first opportunity. Or maybe just abandon it in a desert somewhere. She hadn't said anything to the others about their unexpected passengers. When she came back and Tom asked her why she looked like that, she just said, "Like what," and when he said, "Like you've just seen a ghost," she just said, "I always look like this," and he gave up and dropped it. She didn't want to talk about it, and anyway, they were pulling into Achnashellach station.

Kate stepped down onto the platform in the evening gloom, fizzing with nervous anticipation. This was it, this was where the mystery trail led. She was wearing her conductor's outfit in case for some reason she needed to look official.

But there was no one here to look official for. The station lights were all off, and the platform was empty. Insects chirped softly and slowly. Kate peered nervously into the Scottish darkness.

"In the movies," Tom whispered, "this would turn out to be a trap."

Kate couldn't disagree. She hoped this was one of those times when life wasn't like a movie.

"Don't worry," the cassowary said. "There are no dangerous land animals in Scotland."

"Really? No wolves? No bears?"

"Locally extinct. Scottish people are very effective hunters."

"Okay."

"Though there are adders."

"Okay," Tom said.

"And ticks. And Scottish people."

"We're going to go over here now," Kate said.

She and Tom walked down to the far end of the platform. The light from the *Silver Arrow*'s headlight was quickly swallowed up by the gloom. The smooth cement underfoot was littered with pine cones.

"Uncle Herbert?" she called.

She didn't even know what she was looking for. There were no clues here, and precious few non-clues.

"I hate this place," said a voice behind her.

"Oh, come on!" Tom said.

It was the wolverine, ambling along the platform, sniffing the air.

"I couldn't leave him behind," the cassowary said. "He was starving to death."

"I thought he didn't want to come on the train!" Kate said.

"He didn't. I told him I'd step on his head again if he didn't get on."

"Well, as long as he behaves himself."

"Too late for that," said the cassowary. "You should see what he did in the dining car."

"What is it with you?" Kate glared at where she thought the wolverine was in the dimness. "Why can't you behave like a normal person!"

"You mean, why can't I behave like a human?" the wolverine snapped back. "Like a bald-faced, top-heavy ape? Because I'm a wild animal!"

Kate didn't answer that, because the wolverine was right—that was what she'd meant, she did want him to act like a human. And yet that didn't seem fair. The wolverine stopped and sniffed the air again. Out in the wild like this, he cut a more impressive figure than he had back in Uncle Herbert's apartment.

He looked alert and aggressive, head held high, with huge, heavy, floofy paws and an air of savage strength just barely held in check.

"Something's wrong here," he growled.

"Wrong? Like how?"

"Sh!" Then more quietly: "This place isn't right. It's out of balance."

"What do you mean?"

As far as Kate could tell, it was just a cool Scottish night in a quiet pine forest. Empty and eerie, maybe, but she wouldn't have said *unbalanced*. But the wolverine stood at attention like a hunting hound who's scented the quarry. Then like a shot he bounded off the platform and into the dark woods.

"Stay here," Kate said to Tom.

"Why?"

"Because backup!"

If she'd been more truthful and had more time, she might have told him that she didn't think he could take care of himself and she didn't want the distraction of worrying about him. But for now she dove into the trees after the

The Golden Swift

wolverine, arms in front of her face to keep from getting scratched. Probably there was a flashlight somewhere aboard the *Silver Arrow*, but there was no time for that now. *It's a miracle humans ever find anything at all*, she thought. *Would it have killed us to evolve some night vision? Or just a decent sense of smell?*

But then Kate did see something up ahead, a glimmer of golden light through the branches of the black trees. She stopped running and crouched down.

It was a train, halted on the track a few hundred yards past the station. Steam leaked from the engine—you could see it drifting in the harsh electric light. One of the Great Secret Intercontinental Railway trains, it had to be. In fact, Kate was pretty sure she recognized this one, because she'd seen it before, quite recently, at way too close range. It was the *Golden Swift*.

The door of one of the passenger cars opened, spilling yellow light out into the night. Kate's eyes narrowed as four big cats loped out, one after the other, with their cool loose-shouldered gait, and flowed off into the darkness together. For a second she thought one of them might be her dear old friend the fishing cat, and her heart leaped....

But no, the fishing cat was far away, safe in a mangrove swamp on the other side of the world, with her funny webbed paws and her dear olive-green coat. And these cats were bigger. As much as she loved her, the fishing cat was not a very big cat.

"What are they?" she whispered.

"Lynx," the wolverine said. "You ignorant screen-staring monkey. We hunt them."

"You *eat* those things?!"

"Delicious."

"That is just—! Who would eat a—? Never mind! What are they doing here?"

"Nothing good," the wolverine said. "They shouldn't be here. There are no lynx in Scotland. I told you, this place is out of balance."

Kate had seen this kind of thing before, and the white-bellied heron had explained how it worked. Sometimes a species would find its way into an eco-system where it didn't evolve, where it had no natural predators, and the native species didn't know how to defend themselves against it. Then it would just eat and eat and multiply and multiply till it was the only thing left. Invasive species threw everything out of balance.

They were always trying to shove their way onto the *Silver Arrow*. But this was different; the *Golden Swift* was actively *helping* the lynx invade. A flame of righteous outrage flared inside her.

"Hey!" She thrashed her way out of the woods and into the glare of the *Golden Swift*'s headlight. "Hey! What are you doing?"

Kate went into full conductor mode, using her authority-figure voice and her authority-figure stride. She caught a glimpse of someone in the passenger car, but then the door slammed shut, steam blasted everywhere, and she heard the brakes snap off. The *Golden Swift* began rolling forward.

"I said hey! Stop! Stop!"

One thing about steam trains: When they started moving, they didn't exactly peel out. They accelerated at a stately, sensible pace, slow and steady. The *Silver Arrow* could do a ferocious clip when it got going, but the getting-going took a good five minutes at least. Which meant that Kate could, with a little agility, grab on to something and hop aboard the *Golden Swift*.

But she hesitated. These were the people who'd kidnapped her uncle. They could be dangerous. They could have guns. Kate was dying to get to the bottom of this; she was *going* to get to the bottom of it, and fix it, and stop what was going on. And she was *so close* to doing it.

But what if what happened to Uncle Herbert happened to her? She stood there, fisting and unfisting her hands, biting her lip, as car after car of the *Golden Swift* rolled past her. *The Great Secret Intercontinental Railway does have its enemies.*

She couldn't do it. Not alone anyway. Kate turned and ran for the *Silver Arrow*.

The Game Is Afoot

"GO GO GO GO GO!"

Kate was yelling it even as she ran back through the dark woods toward the station. She didn't care now about the twigs and branches whapping her in the face and slashing at her arms. She was not letting these people get away. This was it, this was the key to the mystery. She yanked herself up into the cab.

The *Silver Arrow* wasn't moving.

Tom spun slowly on his stool.

"Where are we going?"

"Just go!" she shrieked. "Go go go! I'll explain on the way!"

If heads could explode, Kate was pretty sure hers would have. Her hands were flying over the controls.

OKAY, OKAY

The *Silver Arrow* began to move. Usually Kate found this part deliciously satisfying, but now she felt like she was going to die from impatience. Would it help if she got out and pushed? Why oh why did they have to pick so many cars? Couldn't they just leave a few here? Like maybe the one with horrible stinging bees in it? Kate explained as fast as she could what was going on, what she'd seen and why it was so important. Then she had to explain it again, more slowly, because apparently the first time she'd been talking so fast that nobody understood her.

Click-*bing*.

I DON'T KNOW IF WE CAN CATCH THEM

"What? Of course you can!"

"Not with that attitude," Tom said as he rotated.

"They've got a minute or two head start, that's all! Tom, shovel!"

Tom got to his feet, stuck a shovel into the pile of coal, and flicked a few nuggets into the firebox.

"Not like that!"

She grabbed the shovel and started madly flinging coal into the flames. She was almost crying with frustration. Her last connection to Uncle Herbert, her last chance to do something, anything, was slipping away, and they were *dawdling*!

"*SA*, where's your competitive spirit?"

"SA"?

SO I HAVE A NICKNAME NOW?

"Yes! No! I don't know! Just go faster!"

"*TSA*" WOULD BE BETTER

THE SILVER ARROW

"Or just 'the 'Row,'" Tom said. "You know, like short for *Arrow*?"

"Go faster or I will stick this shovel up your steam pump!"

Then Kate had a brainstorm.

"Or you know what? Don't."

She said it almost casually. She put down the shovel.

"Don't even try." Tom frowned at her, confused, but Kate kept going. "That's probably what they're counting on. I bet that train thinks you have no chance of catching it. Probably it thinks you're just a piece of old-fashioned, obsolete scrap."

There was a pause.

WHAT DO YOU MEAN BY THAT EXACTLY

"Oh, nothing," Kate said airily. "I just figure that with all that newfangled aerodynamic styling it's got, the *Golden Swift* probably has a pretty high opinion of itself. Probably it thinks you're too embarrassed to try to catch it."

THAT'S JUST A LOT OF FANCY SHEET METAL

"Looks pretty cool, though." Tom was catching on. "It's probably an A4 class. I hear they're pretty speedy."

The *Silver Arrow* snorted steam.

ALL FLASH

"It's got a double chimney, too," Tom went on. "Did you notice? And probably one of those Kyl-chap exhausts. Improves the efficiency. It's the little things, you know?"

IT IS *NOT* THE LITTLE THINGS

IT'S THE BIG THINGS! LIKE MY ENORMOUS POWERFUL ENGINE!

"If only there were some way," Kate said, "to find out which one of you is faster…"

DON'T THINK I DON'T KNOW WHAT YOU'RE DOING

But it didn't matter. Now it was really on.

Tom and Kate shoveled for all they were worth, and there was a lot of very technical back-and-forth among all three of them about how hot the firebox could safely go, and what pressure the boiler could stand, and where to set the cutoff valve, and how fast they could go around turns without derailing, and so on. They shot through the Scottish night, trees and bridges and signals and tunnels whipping by in the darkness, and Kate had that amazing feeling she sometimes got, like she was riding this massively powerful machine down rails of slick ice, so fast and slippery that nothing could stop them.

The sound of the *Golden Swift*'s whistle drifted back to them through the night air. Cheeky! Though it wasn't till then that it occurred to Kate to wonder what exactly they would do if they caught up with them.

It wasn't like they could just order the *Golden Swift* to pull over. Several impractical schemes flashed through her head, including: somehow jumping from the nose of the *Silver Arrow* to the *Golden Swift*'s caboose (pro: heroically dangerous; con: what would she do next?); somehow hitching the front of the *Arrow* to the *Swift*'s caboose, then throwing the *Arrow* into reverse and dragging them to a halt (pro: less dangerous; con: probably impossible); or just straight-up ramming them (pro: dramatic; con: they would explode and everyone would die).

But she couldn't let them get away. She just couldn't.

With an almighty *slam*, the *Silver Arrow* blew through a junction and raced off down a branch line, rocking back and forth on the rails with the force of the turn. But the *Golden Swift* hadn't turned, it was still on the main line, and its lights immediately dwindled away behind them through the trees and disappeared.

"What are you doing?!" Kate shouted. "You're losing them!"

NO I'M NOT

"Yes! You are!"

"Where are we going?" Tom yelled.

SOMEWHERE THEY DON'T KNOW ABOUT

Kate could see why they wouldn't, because the *Silver Arrow* now appeared to be barreling through trackless swamps, flat expanses of stagnant water and mudflats reflecting a full moon. Out of nowhere a hill loomed up, and Kate threw up an arm to ward off the inevitable crash, but instead they shot into a tunnel, and a rush of darkness swallowed them.

In rapid succession they sped through a huge, empty station, across a frozen snowy plain, along a beach of black sand, and over a high bridge of steel trestles.

"What's happening?!" Kate shouted over the roar of the wind and the engine.

THE GREAT SECRET INTERCONTINENTAL RAILWAY

IS NOT SIMPLY A BUNCH OF TRACKS

IT'S A NETWORK OF CONSTANTLY SHIFTING DIMENSIONAL SHUNTS AND BYPASSES

OBEYING A MYSTICAL GEOMETRY THAT ONLY
THE MOST GIFTED CAN GRASP

"I feel like you're going to tell us that you are among those gifted few."

I'M NOT GOING TO TELL YOU

I'M GOING TO SHOW YOU

Then the *Silver Arrow* snapped on its brakes.

The night around them was absolutely still. A clear, bright moon hung overhead, and around it the stars blazed the way they only did when you were far, far away from any city. They were in a great desert by a dark ocean—out the left-hand window Kate could see nighttime surf breaking on sand, while on the right an infinity of smooth overlapping dunes stretched away into the distance.

The waves were the only thing that moved. A warm night breeze blew through the cab. The air was so dry that Kate could feel the water evaporating off her skin.

NOW WE HAVE THEM

"We do?"

Far away on the horizon, a light appeared. It looked like a firefly or a falling star.

"Is that the *Golden Swift*?" Tom said.

First it was just a point. Then it was a spark, then as it came closer and turned toward them, following the empty coastline, it sprouted beams. It was coming fast, and the closer it got, the more obvious it became that they were on the same track. It was a collision course, just like last time, only this time they were stopped dead. Nowhere to run.

IT'S ALL IN THE TIMING

"What do you mean by 'it,' exactly?" Kate asked nervously.

THREE

TWO

ONE

The *Silver Arrow* switched on its headlight. Instantly there was a distant answering flare of sparks from underneath the oncoming train as it threw its brakes on full. A moment later, traveling at the speed of sound, which is slower than light, there came the faraway shriek of steel on steel as the *Golden Swift* went from charging full steam ahead to desperately skidding along the tracks, trying to stop.

"Wouldn't you have been just a little bit sorry to have missed this?" Kate whispered to Tom.

She stood up. Probably the sanest option would've been to jump out of the car and run as far away as possible as fast as possible. But she didn't.

"Where are we?" she said.

NAMIBIA

THEY CALL THIS THE SKELETON COAST

"I don't think I want to know why they call it that," Tom said.

The *Swift* was closer now; they could make out its golden fuselage in the beam from its headlights and the sparks pouring out from under its wheels. It was slowing down, but it was slowing down slowly. Kate calmly got out of the cab and climbed down to the tracks.

It was utterly desolate country. She strode to the front of the train and sat herself down on the cowcatcher to wait. It's not that she wasn't afraid, but she trusted the *Silver Arrow*. At moments like this she really appreciated what true friends they were, even if the *Silver Arrow* couldn't trade cat stickers with her. And she trusted that what she was doing was worth the risk. There were other ways to be special besides being up onstage with people cheering for you.

Though she did think that if anyone had been watching, she would've looked pretty cool.

The beautifully rounded front of the *Golden Swift* came looming up out of the night, closer and closer, slower and slower, brakes squealing, till Kate had to shield her eyes with her hand because its lights were so bright. (Unlike the *Silver Arrow*, it had no cowcatcher—Kate supposed it would have ruined that smooth aerodynamic exterior. But how would it catch cows?)

It stopped cold with about ten feet to spare.

Kate sat there motionless, with a coal shovel across her knees. She could hear the chorus of hisses as the other train vented steam. Whoever was in the

cab cut the headlights. Kate could hear them climb down onto the track.

She'd made a mental list of people who she was hoping the driver of the *Golden Swift* would *not* turn out to be. Hitler. Darth Vader. Ms. Tinkler. A wild boar. Some weird, evil anti-Kate from another dimension, who would look exactly like her except for a flowing mustache. Robby Vanderveen, who'd hit her in the face once with a ball during dodgeball and only apologized when the gym teacher made him, and he obviously hadn't meant it. She said a silent prayer that it wouldn't be any of those people.

Her prayer came true, but only because she hadn't bothered to put the actual person on the list, because that person never would've occurred to her in a hundred years. He stepped out into the beam of the *Silver Arrow*'s headlight.

"Hello," said Jag. "Or maybe I should say, 'We meet again.'"

The Missing Lynx

AT FIRST KATE DIDN'T REACT. SHE WAS THAT SHOCKED. She stared at him with her mouth open. Whatever speeches she'd been planning just vanished out of her head, cleanly, deleted, just like that.

Jag cleared his throat.

"Maybe I didn't articulate clearly. I said, 'We meet again.'"

"I know," Kate said frostily, "what we are doing again. Why are you here?"

"I could ask you the same question." He looked as unruffled as he had the day of the audition, though now instead of a suit he was wearing the same thing Kate was, namely a conductor's uniform. "But it's rude to answer a question with a question, so I'll go first: I am here, on the west coast of the Republic of Namibia, because you and your steam train chased us here and then—quite cleverly, I must admit—pulled ahead of us and cut us off."

Kate ignored the flattery.

"I think a proper answer to that question would have included an explanation as to why you were in Achnashellach forest just now, releasing non-native animals in violation of everything the Great Secret Intercontinental Railway stands for. And what have you done with Uncle Herbert?"

Now, *that* was a speech. And she'd said it out loud, too. Even if the only audience was just stupid Jag.

"Did you know the name *Achnashellach* comes from a Gaelic phrase meaning 'field of the willows'? Though I didn't see any actual willows there, did you?" Jag had a weird way of talking, like a kid pretending to be a college professor or a member of Congress. Though unlike her he didn't stumble over the name: *Ack-na-SHELL-ack*. "But there I go, answering a question with a question again.

Perhaps you'd like to step into our coffee car while I explain?"

"You have a coffee car?"

Tom had come down from the *Silver Arrow*'s cab, along with the cassowary and the wolverine. Kate still missed her old friends from her first trip, but at this moment she was glad to have two extremely intimidating animals standing behind her.

"We have a tea car, too," Jag said. "Wren doesn't like all the caffeine. Hello, I'm Jag."

"I'm Tom. Are you really allowed to drink coffee?"

"Yes. Aren't you?"

"My parents won't even let me drink a Diet Coke. They think caffeine gives kids anxiety. I snuck some of my dad's coffee once though. It tasted terrible."

"It is something of an acquired taste. We have Diet Coke, too, if you'd prefer. Come."

Just like that, Jag turned and walked back along the track, apparently completely sure that they were going to follow him. Exactly unlike somebody who'd just been caught red-handed committing a serious crime.

And Tom did follow him, without a backward glance. Kate sighed.

"Cassowary, you're with me," she said.

"Right behind you."

"You," Kate snapped at the wolverine, "stay right here. We've got enough problems as it is."

For once the wolverine did as he was told.

Kate had never been inside somebody else's train before, and it was strange, both familiar and different. Where the *Silver Arrow* was all done in dark colors, navy blue and black and Oriental carpets, the *Golden Swift* was decorated in warm yellows and reds and blond woods, and there were skylights overhead. It wasn't what she'd expected. Not in any obvious way a Train of Evil.

Kate and Tom and the cassowary followed Jag into a plush parlor car that smelled powerfully of coffee beans. There were bins of them along one wall, and along the other was a marble counter crammed with elaborate gleaming coffee-making equipment. Jag got busy measuring and pouring and grinding and steaming.

Kate just watched him, glaring, her mind in full rebellion. He had a lead in the school play, and she didn't, and now he got to be a conductor, too? How was that fair?!

"I can only imagine what you thought," he said as he worked. "We probably did look as though we were up to something nefarious. And I suppose in a certain sense we were."

"Okay, first of all, who are 'we'?"

"I think I mentioned Wren. *GS*, where is Wren?"

He picked up what looked like an old-fashioned phone receiver hanging on the wall and listened for a second.

"She's on her way."

"Is that how you talk to your train? A phone?!"

"Of course. How do you talk to yours?"

"I just talk! Like a normal person!"

Just then Wren arrived. She was a girl Tom's age or thereabouts, short and with her blond hair tucked up under her cap in a way that made her look more like a miniature grown-up than a kid. She and Jag were evidently not brother and sister, the way she and Tom were.

"Kate, this is Wren."

"Hi, Kate. Nice work cutting us off."

Wren made a lot of confident eye contact.

"It's nice to meet you." Kate felt like it was important to have good manners in front of your

archenemies. If you were rude they would only use it against you later.

"Hi," said Tom. "I'm Tom."

Wren studied him for a good long second. Then she nodded.

"I think you should come see our trampoline car, Tom." She held open the door. Wren had a straightforward, unbashful way about her that reminded Kate of someone, she couldn't place who, until she realized that Wren reminded her of Tom.

Tom gave Kate a look that said: *Some people think it's okay to have trampoline cars.*

"Don't forget this," Jag called after him.

He tossed Tom a can of Diet Coke, which he'd retrieved from a mini-fridge. Tom caught it. It was like they were all suddenly in a Diet Coke commercial.

"Excuse us for just one moment, won't you?" Kate gave Jag a thin smile and followed Tom out into the corridor.

"What?" he said.

"'What?'" She mimicked him. "What are you doing? These are the bad guys!"

"They don't seem so bad."

"Really? How did they seem when they were releasing lynxes—lynx—whatever—into a Scottish forest? Was that good? No! It was bad!"

"Well, okay," Tom said. "But I'm sure their trampoline isn't bad. Trampolines are innocent. They know nothing of good and evil."

He popped open his Diet Coke.

"Fine," Kate snapped. "I hope you don't have any fun at all with your new best friend!"

She stomped back into the coffee car, fuming. At least the cassowary was still on her side.

"You were telling me how you're not destroying the world." Kate refolded her arms. Jag had now finished making a cup of coffee and was drinking it with irritating pleasure, more or less exactly like her parents did. It felt like a calculated attempt at intimidation.

"We really aren't. I'll explain. But I can't do it in front of the dispatcher."

"What?"

"Nonsense," said the cassowary.

"I'm sorry, I won't discuss it in front of a representative of the Great Secret Intercontinental Railway."

"Why not?" the cassowary asked reasonably.

"I'm a representative of the GSIR," Kate said. "*You're* a representative of the GSIR!"

"Both very good points. But I still can't explain in front of the cassowary. Sorry."

There was the unmistakable scratchy *clack* of the cassowary tapping a talon on the varnished wood floor of the coffee car. She eyed Jag a few seconds longer.

"I'll wait outside," she said finally.

"Thank you."

"I'm only going because I don't consider you a significant threat."

She stalked out into the desert night.

"So." Jag poured himself some more coffee. "You saw us releasing those lynx into the woods."

"You admit it." Kate stared at him stonily.

"You probably don't consider Eurasian lynx native to Scotland."

"Because they aren't."

"But that's the thing: They are. There haven't been any lynx in Scotland for a very long time, but they used to be quite common. For thousands of years lynx were one of Scotland's apex predators, right up until around thirteen hundred years ago, which is when human beings hunted them to extinction."

"So?" Kate narrowed her eyes at him, but inwardly she was turning it over in her head. She hadn't thought of it like that. "But they're not extinct."

"They're extinct *in Scotland*. There are still Eurasian lynx all over Europe. And Asia, as the name would imply. But they disappeared from Scotland. When they did, the effects were catastrophic.

"It works like this." He started pacing up and down the car. "The lynx were at the top of the food chain. They mostly preyed on deer. So what happened when they disappeared? The deer population increased. Which doesn't sound so bad, right? Everybody loves deer. The more deer the better. But!"

Jag put his coffee down so he could wave his wiry arms around as he talked.

"Everything has consequences. What do the deer prey on? Plants. Leaves. Tree shoots. Brambles. Ivy. Herbs. As the deer population got bigger and bigger, they ate more and more, to the point where the plants were having trouble keeping up. The forests started shrinking, nibbled away to nothing by huge herds of hundreds and hundreds of deer.

"And it doesn't end there. Everything has consequences, and those consequences also have consequences. With the forests and meadows disappearing, the animals that lived there began to disappear, too. Squirrels and rabbits and mice and voles. And when they started to go, so did the animals that preyed on *them*, the foxes and pine martens and owls.

"Insects need plants, so when they went, the insect population crashed, too. And what feeds on insects? Birds. Bats. Hedgehogs. They started disappearing. The whole ecosystem suffered. It turns out that everything in nature is connected, and if you pull out one piece, it all starts falling apart.

"But what if we could put it together again. What if we could put the missing piece back?"

He stopped pacing and turned his unexpectedly deep brown eyes on Kate.

"So we took the *GS* to Siberia, where there's plenty of Eurasian lynx. They didn't need much persuading. Who wouldn't want a chance to be top predator again, in a country where herds of deer a thousand strong roam the countryside, just begging to be gobbled up?

"And the lynx remember. They know they belong in Scotland. They know Scotland belongs to them. So we're bringing them back."

One Hundred
Thousand Deer

KATE'S MIND WAS SPINNING FURIOUSLY. SHE WOULD never have thought of this in a thousand years. The idea that Jag could possibly be right about anything irritated her, but if there was something wrong with what he was saying, she wasn't sure what it was.

"So your theory," she said slowly, "is that if you bring the lynx back to Scotland, they'll take care of the deer problem, and nature will find its balance again."

"I don't know." Jag picked up his coffee again. "It's always complicated. But why not? And could things get any worse? Guess how many deer the

Scottish government has to shoot every year, just to keep them under control?"

He waited.

"I don't know. A thousand?" Kate hated when people made her guess things.

"Try a hundred thousand. A hundred thousand deer, every year, just to keep the population under control. Just to keep them from nibbling the whole country down to the roots! But once the lynx start eating the deer instead, they won't have to. Trees

will come back. Forests will come back, then insects, birds, bats, hedgehogs…the whole land will come back to life! Kate, aren't you tired of it?"

"Tired of what?" She also hated it when people used her name in dramatic rhetorical questions.

"Of trying and trying and trying and nothing getting any better?"

Kate didn't say anything. It was a private feeling, one she wasn't ready to talk about with someone like Jag, but of course she was tired of it. She was sick to death of it, and she longed for an answer, something that wouldn't just solve the problem but solve the problem behind the problem, permanently. She wanted it so badly.

"It can't be that simple," she said. "I mean, can you really just go…messing around with nature like that?"

"But that's just it! Nature's already been messed with! We're un-messing it!"

"How much does the GSIR know about this?"

"Not much." For the first time Jag sounded uncomfortable. "I wanted to tell my field agent about it but…I just don't think he'd get it. They're so slow. So cautious. They're still treating the symptoms when we should be going after the root causes.

They're saving individual animals when we should be saving whole ecosystems. We still take assignments from the railway, of course, but the rest of the time we're off doing this."

"So the lynx isn't the first animal you've done this with?"

"It's the fifth!" Jag couldn't keep the boyish pride out of his voice. "Just in the UK, we did sea eagles and beavers, too."

"Beavers?" Kate had always sort of thought of beavers as an American thing. Or at least not a Scottish thing.

"There are supposed to be beavers in Britain! Can you believe it? They went extinct there four hundred years ago—people hunted them for their skins—but they're native animals, just like the lynx, and there are whole ecosystems that need them back. Beaver dams control flooding, and they make wetlands for fish and waterbirds and insects and otters. There are tree species that *evolved* to be gnawed on by beavers, and there's nothing to gnaw on them!

"We're living in a world that is a shambles of what it ought to be. What it used to be. To be honest I'm glad you caught me."

"You are? Why?"

"Because now we can work together!"

Kate hadn't seen that coming.

"Oh," she said. "Thanks. But I work alone. I mean, except for Tom. And the *Silver Arrow*. We're not really joiners."

"But if you guys helped, we could do so much more—!"

"Stop." She held up a hand. "Look—just stop talking for a minute!"

The problem with people like Jag was that they talked faster than Kate could think. They *sounded* so reasonable. But lots of things sounded reasonable. Was this why he'd gotten a part in the musical and she hadn't? Because he was so confident, so assertive, so good at sounding reasonable?

She hadn't planned on this. She'd planned on catching some evildoers red-handed, giving them a good talking-to, and then turning them over to the appropriate authorities, whoever that might be. And rescuing Uncle Herbert. But this was more complicated. This wasn't the solution to the mystery, this was another mystery piled on top of the first one. It was illegal, and irresponsible, and at the same time something about it felt like exactly what she'd been looking for. All she wanted was to save the world. Was that so much to ask?!

And she'd wanted somebody to share all this with,

somebody else who knew about the railroad. Though why did it have to be him? And what did all this have to do with Uncle Herbert?

"What does all this have to do with Uncle Herbert?" she asked.

"I'm afraid I don't know who that is."

"Okay." It was worth a try. "Thanks for all this. I need time to think."

"Take your time," Jag said. "Just please don't tell the cassowary."

Kate picked up the old-timey phone on the wall.

"*Golden Swift*," she said, "please tell the blond goofball in the trampoline car that I need him back on the *Silver Arrow*."

The voice that answered was musical and definitely not human—it sounded like the ringing of crystal chimes, except that the ringing somehow made words.

"*Which blond goofball?*"

"Oh. The boy."

"*Roger that*," it said pleasantly.

So that's what a train sounded like. Huh. She hung up the phone.

"Bye, Jag. I'll see you in school."

When she climbed down out of the *Golden Swift*, the pale surf was still crashing on the sands, the cool desert wind was still sighing, the sand still hissing, the dunes still stretching away into infinity. She'd almost forgotten that they were in the middle of a vast desert, on the edge of the ocean, in the Republic of Namibia.

The cassowary was still patiently waiting for her, too.

"What did you learn?" she asked.

"That the lynx remember," Kate said. "If you need me, I'll be in my Slumberliner."

A Terrible, Terrible Thing

SO FAR KATE HAD SUCCESSFULLY ENLISTED A CASSO-
wary, acquired a new set of train cars, found her uncle
Herbert's secret invisible apartment, deciphered a
clue, liberated a wolverine, outwitted a rival train, and
interrogated its conductor. So far, so not bad.

But she couldn't think of what to do next. The
trail had gone cold. She'd run out of clues. So, reluctantly, she went where she went when all else failed:
back to school.

She didn't think about Jag's scheme for bringing
back missing animals, and she didn't *not* think about
it, either. She just let it sit there, in the back of her

mind, rattling around, till she could figure out what to make of it.

Meanwhile there was plenty to occupy the front of her mind. She was in middle school now, and her first life, her real life, was a lot more complicated than it used to be. There was homework, and tests, and cliques, and locker combinations, and where-to-sit-at-lunch, and hallway-crushes-that-lasted-five-minutes. There were after-school rehearsals for *Anything Goes*. Kate didn't have to show up every day, BECAUSE SHE WAS ONLY IN THE CHORUS. But the chorus was in a lot of scenes, and the closer they got to the big night, the more often she had to go.

Though the funny thing about being in the chorus was that she didn't really mind it, or not nearly as much as she'd thought she would.

It was the exact opposite of what she'd thought

she wanted, but the truth was, it was kind of a relief to be out of the spotlight for a change. On the *Silver Arrow* everything depended on her. Everybody looked to her for what to do next. But in the chorus she had the fun of being up onstage in front of an audience without the pressure of being in charge. She really wasn't all that good at singing—yet—and her dancing was even more of a work in progress, but it didn't matter. Nobody cared. When she messed up, she and the other chorus kids just laughed about it and tried again.

Maybe this was why she'd tried out. She'd thought she wanted to be the star, the hero, but maybe what she really wanted was just to have normal human friends who talked about their dogs and played soccer and made jewelry on weekends. And traded cat stickers.

Of course Jag was there too, but he and Kate didn't talk to each other. She just nodded to him when they passed, coolly, as if to say, *Our secret lives might be connected, but that doesn't mean our real lives are.* Sometimes Kate would stand in the darkened wings of the stage, with the heavy ropes and dusty old props and a big piece of sheet metal they used to make thunder sound effects, and she'd watch Jag do his big numbers and say his corny dialogue. She had to admit that he was pretty good at the singing. Maybe less good at the corny dialogue.

Meanwhile the bushfires were still burning in Australia. Studies were saying that more than a billion animals had been killed or had lost their habitats. She wondered about all that stuff Jag had told her about, that he and Wren and the *Golden Swift* were doing. Would it really work? She did some poking around on the internet, and it turned out Jag wasn't the first person who'd thought of it. There was a famous example about bringing wolves back to Yellowstone Park. In the 1920s the wolves had been systematically eliminated by park rangers, but then in the 1990s they decided to bring them back, mostly because the local elk populations were getting out of hand.

The wolves helped with the elk problem, but there were all kinds of other consequences too. Just for example, elk eat young willows, so fewer elks meant that there were more willow trees in the park. Beavers like willows, so when the trees grew back that meant that beavers came back to Yellowstone, too. Which meant more wetlands, which meant more habitats for otters and minks and wading birds and even moose… It was a chain reaction. The consequences had consequences. Kate still didn't know whether what Jag was doing was right or wrong or just plain weird. But could it be more wrong than what she was doing now, which was nothing?

And it was exciting. I mean, Kate had a secret double life, but Jag had a secret life *inside his secret double life.*

Though for somebody who was basically a triple agent, Jag didn't exactly radiate coolness. Kate would be the first to admit that she wasn't exactly the queen of the school, but Jag was exceptionally unpopular. Apparently—Kate's new friends in the chorus told her—he'd been homeschooled up until this year, so he'd come in not knowing anybody and just not really being used to regular school.

Which was a bummer, but he seemed to be determined to make the worst of a tough situation. He talked a little too precisely and formally, as if he'd spent most of his life as the only kid in the room, trying to fit in with the grown-ups. He liked to make long speeches in class, and he got impatient when people didn't understand him, and he wasn't careful about showing it—he had a way of lifting his chin and looking down at you while he talked. He ignored social cues, and he had the kind of eccentric mannerisms that have usually rubbed off by the time you got to sixth grade: He stood up too straight and never looked to the left or right when he walked, just stared straight ahead.

Also he only ever wore white button-down shirts, which he always kept tucked in. None of this stuff was a problem out on the Great Secret Intercontinental Railway, but it didn't fly in middle school. As far as Kate could tell, Jag had no friends at all. He didn't seem to want any.

Bullies liked him, though. Kate had always thought bullies were attracted to kids who cried easily or got angry—anyone they could get a reaction out of, basically—and that was probably true, but bullies were attracted to Jag for the opposite reason. He never reacted. Whatever people said or did, he just waited it out, without crying or fighting back or yelling for a teacher. As a result the mean kids liked to see how far they could push him.

One day Jag brought in a project he'd done for

social studies, a papier-mâché model of a mountain all covered with meticulous little trees made out of snips of green pipe cleaner. It was too big to fit in his locker, so he just lugged it around with him all day. It turned into a running gag: Everywhere he went—in class, in the halls, at lunch—kids would bump into Jag's model mountain, or spill things on it, or knock it out of his hands. Then they would make elaborate fake apologies and pretend to try to help him pick it up but drop it again and step on it instead. By the time lunch rolled around, Jag's green landscape was almost completely deforested, and it looked like it had been the victim of some violent volcanic event or meteor strike, too.

Kate knew she should say something or do something to help him. But she couldn't quite figure out what exactly, and whenever she thought about it, her mind just came up with more and more reasons not to do anything. Maybe Jag would be embarrassed to have her come to his defense. Maybe she would only make things worse by attracting attention.

But the real truth was that she was afraid. She was afraid that helping Jag would make her unpopular like he was. That her new friends in the chorus would stop liking her. Kate didn't want to help Jag, but she didn't want to be a coward, either.

After lunch Kate was heading for math class when she spotted Jag in the library, sitting by himself, with his model on the table in front of him. He'd turned it over and was trying to repair it from below with industrial quantities of masking tape, though it wasn't clear whether he was making matters better or worse.

She watched him for a minute. Here in the school library he looked very vulnerable and helpless. Very different from how he looked lounging in his coffee car on the *Golden Swift*.

She went across the hall to the art teacher Mrs. Zavala's classroom, which was mercifully empty, and commandeered a box of colored pencils, some glue, and some cotton balls. Then she went back to the library and sat down opposite Jag. He had apparently given up on repairing the volcanic disaster and was just sitting there staring at his ruined model.

Sometimes Kate wished she wasn't quite such a good person. Having a conscience made you do some terrible, terrible things.

"I don't know if there's a God or not," Jag said, "but if there is then I feel sorry for him because making a mountain is a lot harder than it looks."

"And you only had to make one. He had to make like a million."

Kate took a brown pencil from Mrs. Zavala's box and made a dot on the mountainside.

"What's that?" Jag said.

"It's a deer."

He squinted at it.

"What's it doing there?"

Kate was already making more little brown dots.

"It's part of a herd. They're overgrazing. That's what happened to all your trees. Or you can explain to Mr. Zhang that Amanda Oldfarm sat on it, but I don't think that's going to help your grade any."

"But it's supposed to be Lookout Mountain. It's in Tennessee."

"Not anymore, now it's the Scottish Highlands."

Kate kept going. The deer were reproducing rapidly.

"That wasn't the assignment."

"It's too late for that. You're going to explain to everybody about all that stuff you told me. Extinction and lynxes and how it led to a tragic decline in pine martens or whatever."

Hesitantly Jag picked up another brown pencil, a slightly lighter one, and started adding deer, too. "What are we going to do about that crushed part?"

"What happened there?"

"Ted Azarello stepped on it."

"Ted Azarello."

"I believe that was his name."

"Jag," Kate said, "I'm the first person to admit that popularity is not all there is to life, but when Ted Azarello is stepping on your social studies project, I'm going to have to put my hand up and say that you might think about working on your interpersonal skills a tiny little bit."

Jag pursed his lips. Kate allowed herself a little satisfaction at being the one who was doing the lecturing for a change.

"But to answer your question," she went on, "we're going to cover the crushed part with this." She started pulling the cotton balls into thin shreds. "It's smoke from a wildfire. A rampaging wildfire that is consuming the Scottish Highlands, as a result of drought and unseasonably high temperatures. We'll just stick it on with some glue. See?"

It really did look sort of like the footage of wildfires that was always on TV. Jag picked up an orange pencil and started adding some fire.

"In a way I like this better than what I had before." His spirits were coming back. "I mean, even before Amanda Oldfarm sat on it."

"I think you can take it from here." Kate stood up. "I have to get to math."

"I'm just worried, though." Jag was busily

applying smoke to the Highlands now. "The assignment was to make a model of an important battle site from the Civil War."

"You'll just have to explain to Mr. Zhang that sometimes the present is more urgent than the past. The Civil War was bad but we have more pressing problems right now."

"You really think he'll accept that?"

"As a great woman once observed," Kate said, "sometimes it's better to ask forgiveness than permission."

With that, she went to math.

The Hero and the Villain

A COUPLE OF DAYS LATER KATE FOUND A FOLDED-UP piece of paper in her locker—it must have been slipped in through the slots in the door. Her heart clenched when she saw it. It was that same kind of thick creamy paper that Uncle Herbert always left for her....

But it wasn't from Uncle Herbert. It was an official timetable for the Great Secret Intercontinental Railway, but it wasn't for the *Silver Arrow*. It was for the *Golden Swift*.

She tracked Jag down during lunch. He was sitting by himself, as usual, eating an apple.

"I thought maybe you would want to make the stops instead of me," he explained, with his usual maddening calm.

"Why would you think that?" Kate didn't see why Jag thought he was in the business of knowing anything about her or what she might or might not want.

"Because I know how much you care about the work that the railway does."

"And why would you think *that*?"

"Because when you caught me releasing lynx at Achnashellach, you chased me all the way to Namibia. That's why. But I can do the stops myself if you'd rather."

He was right, she really did want that timetable. She wanted to get back out on the *Silver Arrow*. She didn't like the idea of being in debt to him, but she guessed he was in debt to her already, so this would just make it even.

"Fine. I'll do it."

She turned to go. Then she turned back.

"Thank you."

"You're welcome," Jag said.

"What did you get on your Civil War project?"

"An A. Also Mr. Zhang canceled the Civil War unit and is making everybody do a project on the social consequences of climate change instead."

As it turned out, Kate was glad she took the timetable. She'd forgotten how much she loved all the little technical details of running the train, and the pleasure of being precisely on time, and of meeting an absurd variety of bizarre animals. She loved just reading the place names: the Miombo woodlands; the Sundarbans, which was the world's biggest mangrove forest; the Monteverde cloud forest; the Yellow River mudflats. In the Valdivian rain forest, a tiny wildcat called a kodkod boarded the train. It was no bigger than a house cat.

In a quiet meadow in Belgium, she picked up an animal that she would've thought was an unusually athletic-looking guinea pig but who indignantly identified herself as a critically endangered European hamster instead. Kate hadn't realized there were actual, real non-pet hamsters out there living in the wild; her surprise prompted an operatic speech on the eighteen(!) different species of hamster, of which the European hamster was proud to be the largest and most aggressive (though Kate didn't really see how "most aggressive hamster" could be a very competitive category).

In the Amazon she picked up a turtle called a matamata, which was the weirdest turtle, and possibly the weirdest animal, she had ever seen. He was definitely the bumpiest animal she'd ever seen. The matamata explained that he was trying to camouflage himself as a heap of dead leaves, and Kate could only congratulate him on his commitment to the role.

Everywhere she went Kate looked for signs of Uncle Herbert. Every animal she met she questioned for clues or leads, but no one knew anything, or at least no one would admit to knowing anything. It wasn't that they acted suspiciously, exactly, and maybe it was just her new detective mode getting the better of her, but sometimes Kate had a curious feeling like maybe she wasn't getting the whole story. As if the mood among the animals had subtly changed. It made her think about what the wolverine had said. If humans were causing all the trouble, how deeply could we really expect animals to trust us?

At one stop a herd of elephants was gathered at the station. They weren't waiting for the train. They just stood there, watching. Kate was relieved that they didn't want to get on, because that was a whole lot of elephants, but something about the way their wise ancient eyes followed her made her uneasy.

It made her feel lonely, too. The cassowary and

the wolverine had stayed behind in the Rail Yard. Tom had said he would come but only to use the dojo car—Tom and Wren had had quite the bonding experience that day in the trampoline car, and it turned out she was taking classes in Muay Thai and was keen to do some sparring, so Tom was brushing up on his moves. These days it seemed like he had a lot more in common with Wren than with Kate. She'd said, *If that's all you're going to do then don't come at all*, and they'd had a fight about it, and he'd gone to his room and slammed the door.

So in between stops Kate wandered back through the cars by herself. She skirted the garden car—she would've liked to give it back to the Rail Yard, but she hadn't had a chance yet—then she read for a while in the library. Then she fooled around in the observatory car for a while. The telescope was so complicated and technical that you had to read a thick binder of procedures and protocols before you could even look through it. She decided in favor of just randomly fiddling with the dials and buttons instead.

She wasn't entirely sorry when she was interrupted. It was the kodkod, the tiny wildcat, who explained that she'd been napping and missed her stop.

"It happens," Kate said. "Let's go talk to the *Silver Arrow*."

The little cat followed her forward through the train. She was outrageously cute and also a little bit hilarious. With her spotted fur and tiny fierce gaze, she looked like a leopard that had somehow been miniaturized but hadn't quite realized it yet. The *Silver Arrow* wasn't very sympathetic to the kodkod's plight, and they were getting into a three-way argument about it when they arrived at their next stop and they all got distracted.

The platform had an old-fashioned-looking brick station house with a blue-green copper dome on top. It was set in a dense, tangled green forest. In the distance the trees gave out onto open wetlands, where a pair of white-necked cranes were stalking through the shallows. Kate stuck her head out the window in time to see two dignified black bears exit the passenger car and lumber off into the mist and the trees.

There was a strange sense of utter stillness and at the same time utter wildness. In the far distance, along a ridgeline beyond the swampland, ran a tall fence topped by a string of yellow lights.

"Where are we?" she said.

WE'RE INSIDE THE KOREAN DEMILITARIZED ZONE

"That's the least picturesque name I've ever heard," Kate said, "for a very picturesque place."

"Oh, I've heard of this. It's famous!" The kod-kod leaped up onto Tom's empty stool and put her paws up on the window. "There was a civil war here, and by the time it was over the two sides hated each other so much that they had to put a strip of land between them to separate them. It runs all the way across the country, coast to coast. No one's been allowed in it for seventy years—there are big barbed-wire fences along either side. So it's all gone back to nature."

You could almost feel it in the atmosphere: the absence of human beings. Nothing trimmed or cropped or sprayed or cleared or trampled or lit-tered. This was how nature was when it was alone and could just be itself. They'd rewilded the whole landscape by accident.

"There's something ironic about this that I'm trying to put my finger on," Kate said.

MAYBE IT'S THAT SOMETIMES WAR FOR HUMANS MEANS PEACE FOR ANIMALS?

"I guess that was it."

"There's other places like this," the kodkod said. "In France there's a place called the Red Zone,

where some of the worst battles of World War One were fought. A hundred years later the ground is still so full of poison gas and unexploded bombs and grenades that no people can live there. But animals do.

"We love anywhere without humans. Chemical spills, failed developments, abandoned docklands— it doesn't matter how bad the damage is, so long as there's no people there. In Russia there's a place called the Chernobyl Exclusion Zone where a nuclear reactor exploded. Everybody had to be evacuated because of the radiation, and they thought the animals would all die, but we haven't. Now the place is full of bears, bison, lynx, wolves, moose, eagles, all kinds of rare species."

"But how's that possible? Isn't the radiation bad for them?"

"It's not great. But it's not as bad as humans. There's a horse species called Przewalski's horse that's so endangered that for years there were only a handful left, and they were all in zoos. But now at Chernobyl, Przewalski's horse has come back in the wild."

The *Silver Arrow* moved on...but Kate's thoughts didn't. They stayed behind in the Korean Demilitarized Zone. It was hard to accept that at the end of the day humans were even worse than land mines and radiation and toxic chemicals. Why couldn't people live without destroying things? And at the same time, it was amazing the way nature always came back. It made her think of those missing lynx, and the beavers, and the wolves in Yellowstone. It made her think of swifts, too—the way they could fly and fly and never land. If only humans could live like that, touching nothing.

Sometimes Kate felt like she was trapped in a story where she didn't know if she was the hero or the villain. She wanted to be the good guy, but she kept turning into the bad guy.

There had to be another way.

"*Silver Arrow*," she said. "I think we need to find the *Golden Swift*."

A Dish of Beetles

"YOU HAVE AN OFFICE CAR?"

"Don't you?" Jag said. "I couldn't keep track of anything without it."

Like the rest of the *Golden Swift*, the office car was bright and airy, with a snazzy Scandinavian-looking desk and a whole wall of neat little drawers and pigeonholes, all of which were stuffed with paper. Jag was pacing and sipping a coffee. This wasn't Hapless Homeschool Jag. He'd gone back to being Secret Intercontinental Jag again, brimming with caffeine and confidence.

"I feel like all this would be easier with a computer," Kate said.

"It definitely would. But the *GS* doesn't like them."

"I thought the *GS* was supposed to be all modern and aerodynamic."

"It is modern," Jag said. "By the standards of about 1938."

Jag rubbed his hands together and started hunting through the pigeonholes on the wall. Each one had a little handwritten label with the name of a species on it. CHEETAH. BROWN HYENA. DARWIN'S RHEA. RED-TAILED PHASCOGALE. WESTERN JAVAN EBONY LANGUR.

"Now, these are all animals where they went extinct in one place but there's still others somewhere else in the world, and the place where they went extinct needs them back. Now that you're here, we have double the person- and train-power, so I've been thinking about what the best next step is—"

Jag was still talking, but as he talked it occurred to Kate that if they were going to do this, she didn't want it to be a deal where he thought he was in charge and she just went around doing what he said. It was Jag's idea, and she was happy to be here, but she wasn't here to take orders. She thought it might be best if she was clear about that up front.

So she walked over to the wall of files and plucked one out at random without looking.

"Let's start with this one."

Jag stopped talking. "Are you sure?"

"I'm sure."

He peered at the file. "How much do you know about the American burying beetle?"

"I figure it's pretty much there in the name."

"Do you know what it is that burying beetles bury?"

Kate's number one fear in that moment was that burying beetles buried poo, so she was relieved when it turned out they didn't. Although not that relieved. What they buried were the corpses of small animals.

According to Jag's file, the story of the American burying beetle was that it used to be all over the United States, but lately there had been fewer and fewer every year.

They were rather handsome-looking bugs, black with prominent orange blotches on their backs. The life goals of an American burying beetle were mostly focused on finding the bodies of dead birds and squirrels and so on that were lying on the ground. Then they went looking for a mate. Then the happy couple would bury the corpse together and make some baby burying beetles, which would eat the corpse and dig their way back up to the surface, and the whole cycle would start over.

You couldn't call it glamorous, but it was important because it helped with breaking down dead things and bringing their nutrients back into the soil. Kate had assumed that that's what worms were for, but apparently it takes a village of creepy-crawly things to deal with a corpse. No one knew exactly why American burying beetles were disappearing, but there were plenty of suspects: climate change, light pollution, habitat loss, pesticides.

Also what burying beetles really liked feeding on was passenger pigeons, which there weren't a lot of these days, since they'd gone extinct about a hundred years ago. Sigh.

Kate had never spoken to an insect before, unless

she counted the bees in the garden car, which she preferred not to think about. She wasn't even clear on whether insects could talk like other animals. But it turned out they could, though their voices were extremely tiny and high, and it was hard to hear them over the rattle of the train. They collected a dozen pairs of burying beetles from around the Midwest—Kansas, Oklahoma, Nebraska, Arkansas. The beetles looked a little lost sitting on the regular seats of the train, where they were in constant danger of being sat on, so Jag fetched a serving dish from the dining car, and they all sat together on that.

The *Swift* took them to a small island off the coast of Massachusetts, a low, grassy scrap of land ringed with rocky beaches, where the beetles could live and build up a population in relative safety. Kate carried the dish out into the quiet salty night air—burying beetles are nocturnal. She tried to keep an open mind about the fact that she was holding a dish full of bugs in the dark. After all, they weren't unpleasant little fellows. With their glossy, boldly spotted carapaces, they might have been a display case of expensive brooches. Though she still worried they would suddenly decide to crawl up her arms and into her hair.

They chatted and chirped quietly among themselves. She put the plate down in the middle of a
meadow. Jag was standing by with a bulging sack.

"Dead pigeons," he explained.

Kate suppressed a shudder. "Where did you even
get them?"

"Wolverine caught them."

Together she and Jag performed the not-very-nice
task of placing the dead pigeons in various suitable
spots around the wide, boulder-strewn field. Each
beetle couple would get a bird. When she was done,
she went back for the dish. But when she placed the
first pair on the ground, they called out something.

"What was that?"

She got down on her knees and bent over them so she could hear, holding back her hair with one hand.

"Could you dig the hole for us?" one of the beetles said.

"I sort of thought you'd want to do that yourselves," Kate said.

"But we don't. We want you to do it."

Well. Kate guessed if she were faced with the extinction of her entire species, she'd feel entitled to some pampering, too. They fetched shovels from the *Golden Swift*. They were coal shovels, not much good for digging, but she and Jag spent the next hour scraping out a dozen little holes and then popping a dead pigeon into each one.

Then they carefully placed the beetles in the holes.

"Now cover us up!" the beetles said.

"Wait, you *are* burying beetles, right?" Jag said. "We didn't get the wrong kind?"

The beetles just waited. So Kate and Jag softly, carefully heaped soil over the beetles and pigeons in their holes.

When they were finally finished and Kate was standing there covered with dirt and sweat but cooling off rapidly, looking out over a midnight meadow on some island off the coast of New England that she couldn't have found with a map or probably even a GPS-enabled mobile device, she realized she felt good. Really good, in a way that she'd been waiting to feel for a long time. She couldn't see them, but out there in the meadow, underground, those twenty-four little beetles were starting their good work, breaking down those dead pigeons into their useful component molecules. Tiny gears in the vast sacred machinery of the natural world were starting to turn. As of tonight the universe was a very little bit less broken.

And she, a human being, had helped. She'd turned back the clock of human destruction just a tick. She wasn't honestly sure if she'd done it to help the world or to make herself feel better, but at that moment it didn't make that much difference to her. Maybe she did feel a little bit better, but was that so wrong? After all, she was part of the world, too.

Arrows and Swifts

KATE LIKED THAT GOOD FEELING. SHE WANTED MORE OF it. So she chased it.

She chased it all the way to China, where she and Jag and Tom and Wren released a herd of curious animals called Père David's deer, which had enormous antlers that looked like tree branches. Père David's deer apparently originally came from China, but they'd all died out there long ago except for a few that were kept by the emperor in the Royal Hunting Garden. Then even those were shot and eaten by German troops during the Boxer Rebellion.

But not before a few specimens were spirited away

by European collectors, and a small herd of them sat out most of the twentieth century at the palatial country estate of some English duke or another. Now it was time for Père David's deer to go back to China, specifically to the Yangtze River basin, where they'd come from in the first place, courtesy of the *Golden Swift* and the *Silver Arrow*.

They took cheetahs to India and condors to Chile and vultures to Bulgaria. They took yellow-bellied toads to Italy. There was a tiny island called Île aux Aigrettes off the coast of Mauritius (which is itself an island off the coast of Madagascar, which is *itself* an island off the coast of Africa—geography!)

that used to have tortoises on it, and a lot of the native plants there had evolved to live with those tortoises. Their fruits needed to be eaten by the tortoises, who would digest the hard outer skins and poo out the seeds, which would then sprout into new plants.

The particular species of tortoise that was native to Île aux Aigrettes had long since been exterminated by heedless European sailors looking for an easy meal that didn't run very fast. But at the end of the day, a tortoise was a tortoise, and there were plenty of other species out there that could eat fruit and poo out seeds with the best of them. Kate and Jag recruited a few—great, taciturn gray beasts like roving hillocks—and took them to Île aux Aigrettes.

Kate felt a little bad that she was doing this behind the back of the Great Secret Intercontinental Railway, which had given her so much. She knew it made the *Silver Arrow* nervous. (She knew this because the *Silver Arrow* complained about it the whole way.) After a lengthy debate with the others, Kate told the cassowary what they were planning. The cassowary said of course she would help. She was only mad that it had taken them so long to ask her.

Even the wolverine wanted in, though only because he was in favor of anything that was against the rules of the Great Secret Intercontinental Railway.

The one person Kate most wanted to talk to about it all was the only one she couldn't, namely Uncle Herbert, because he was still kidnapped, or whatever had happened to him. She felt guilty that they weren't actively looking for him, but she didn't know what else to do. She'd run out of places to look and leads to follow. All she could think of was that somehow by getting deeper into helping the animals, she might be getting closer to what had happened to him. Deeper into the mystery. She hoped it was what he would want her to do.

They brought some fierce, regal, tattered ospreys to Switzerland, where ospreys hadn't lived for a hundred years. They took arctic foxes to Norway. They took some Los Angeles pocket mice out of Los Angeles to somewhere they would be a bit more comfortable. They tried to get some Hine's emerald dragonflies to bring to the woods out behind Kate's house, but they couldn't find any.

They took an entire tribe of giant otters to Argentina. There were twenty of them, and they talked constantly and extremely loudly the entire way—there was some kind of extended-family soap opera going on involving mates and babysitting and grooming that Kate could not, and did not want to, follow closely. The giant otters were unbelievably large, which shouldn't have been surprising given the name, but seriously: measured nose to tail, they were bigger than Kate was. They would've been intimidating if they weren't so chatty.

Theoretically they were related to the wolverine—they were all in the mustelid family—but the wolverine did not emerge to greet his relatives.

But it didn't matter what the animals talked about or what they were like, because whenever Kate watched them slither or slink or bound away from the train into a forest or a field or a placid brown river, she had that same delicious feeling. It was the feeling of snapping a puzzle piece into place, that one piece that had gone missing for ages and that you never thought you'd see again, until suddenly there it was under a couch cushion, and you could finally put it where it belonged.

Or it was like an alarm that had been beeping in the background for Kate's whole life was finally,

finally being turned off. It seemed too good to be true, but there it was, right in front of them. They were doing it. They were putting the world back the way it wanted to be.

They went at it for a solid week, at a grueling pace, going through Jag's files one after another, stopping only to bolt some food or sleep like the dead in their Slumberliners. But that feeling, the feeling that they were finally fixing something and not hurting it, kept them going. That and Jag's coffee, which Kate had sworn never to drink, but after three days of nonstop work, she'd caved. She still hated the taste, and it made her jittery, but it kept her awake.

As they put the world back together, they came together as a team, too, the Arrows and the Swifts. They got scratched and scraped and covered in dirt and sweat and animal hair and less mentionable substances together, and somewhere along the way any instinctive mistrust between them just got worn away, to the point where they could see that underneath it they all cared about the same things. They were none of them natural team players: Kate and Jag were too fond of giving orders, and Tom and Wren were too fond of ignoring them. But once a tapir accidentally headed-butted Kate in the bum, and she yelped—more in surprise than in pain—and the tapir was so startled it pooed, and Jag slipped in the poo and fell on his own bum, and they all collapsed laughing. After that it was hard for anyone to feel like they weren't all in it together.

Jag even let his white shirt finally, finally come untucked.

By the end of the week they were all so exhausted that they were tripping over things and bumping into one another in the halls and forgetting what they were doing in the middle of doing it. They took what they all agreed would be a short break in the dojo car on the *Silver Arrow*, just to recover and plan their next step, but the break kept getting longer and longer.

They lay there sprawled on the floor, staring up at the ceiling, Kate and Tom and Jag and Wren. The wolverine curled up on a practice mat and fell asleep. The cassowary slept, too, looking like a heap of hairy feathers, her blue head bowed and her powerful legs folded under her.

"What's next?" Tom said after a while.

Silence.

"I do not believe that we are accepting new clients at this time," Jag said.

"I believe that our animal-relocation services are temporarily suspended," Kate said.

"I believe," Wren said, "that a pocket mouse has urinated in my pocket."

The rocking of the train made the punching bags sway from side to side over their heads in perfect sync.

"How many more files do we have to go after this?" Kate asked.

"Actually, I think that was all of them," Jag said.

"You're kidding."

"Jag never kids," Wren said.

"When I'm kidding you'll know, because it will be hilarious."

"Does that mean we did the whole world?" Tom said. "Everything's back where it's supposed to be?"

"I wish that were true," Jag said, "but we're not even close. We've barely started."

"And what about the ocean?" Wren said.

"What about it?" said Kate.

"Well, if this has happened on land, then it must've happened in the ocean, too. Shouldn't we be doing something about that?"

"I don't know," Kate said. "I feel like we'd need a submarine for that."

"I have a submarine," Tom said.

The Glass Submarine

"I CAN'T BELIEVE YOU DIDN'T TELL ME YOU HAD A SUB-marine," Kate said for the third time.

"Well," Tom said, "believe it."

They were all in the cab of the *Silver Arrow*, heading back toward the Rail Yard.

"I can't believe you didn't tell me that Tom had a submarine," Kate said to the *Silver Arrow*.

IT WAS A SECRET

"Well, I can't believe you didn't tell me Tom had a secret submarine!"

"Uncle Herbert did say he was going to give me one," Tom said.

"He said he *might* give you one. Anyway, he says lots of things!" A thought struck Kate. "Hang on. Show of hands: How many people here knew that Tom had a submarine?"

Jag and Wren both raised their hands. Kate didn't say anything for a while after that.

The *Silver Arrow* took them back to the Rail Yard, where Tom led Kate and Jag and Wren over to a truly enormous double-length, extra-wide steel car parked on a siding.

Kate still wasn't letting this go. "If I had a secret submarine, or really any kind of submarine, that's all I would talk about ever."

"Well, exactly," Tom muttered.

"What does that mean, 'well, exactly'?"

"It means you always make everything about you."

"What?" That wasn't what she'd been expecting. "No, I don't."

"Yes, you do. You're always doing it." Apparently this was something Tom had been waiting to get off his chest. "Like when you wouldn't let me get a trampoline car."

"It seemed sensible!" Kate said. "At the time! Anyway, you got a whole dojo car!"

"The *Silver Arrow* was supposed to be *our* thing!" Tom's face started getting red. "But you're always giving me orders! Fix this! Shovel that!"

"Well, okay!" Kate found herself getting mad right back. "Uncle Herbert did give it to me, not you. But sure, why don't you try giving orders sometime?"

"I don't know how! It's different for you, it's easy!"

"Easy? For me?!" *Ha!* thought Kate.

"Well, that's how it looks!"

"You have no idea how hard I have to work! I never know what to do, I'm just making it up all the time! And talk about easy—*everything's* easy for you. You want to sing, you just sing. You want friends, you just make friends. You do whatever you feel like whenever you feel like it! Do you have any idea what I would give to be able to do that?"

"What?" Tom planted his hands on his hips.

"Well—a lot!"

"You're just jealous."

"Wait," Kate said. "Is *this* why you haven't been coming on the *Silver Arrow*?!"

Tom didn't answer, but it was written all over his face.

"You will never, *ever* set foot in my submarine," Tom said.

"I think it's great that Tom is expressing his emotions," Jag said.

"Shut up!" Kate and Tom said together.

Tom angrily wiped away tears. Kate's face felt hot, too. If she'd been expressing her own emotions—which she didn't especially feel like doing in front of Jag, or Tom, or really anybody—she probably would've had to admit that Tom was a little bit right. At home she never let Tom into her room, but she walked into his room whenever she felt like it without even asking. She never even thought about it.

And there was the time she'd made him come to Achnashellach when he didn't want to. And then she hadn't let him follow her into the woods when he *did* want to. But he should try doing what she did! He had it so easy! In so many ways!

And he was right, she was jealous of that. And she was supposed to be the big sister.

She took a deep breath and let it out.

"What do you want me to do?"

"I want you to stop acting like you're in charge all the time!"

"Okay." She put her hands on his shoulders and looked him in the eyes. "I promise not to act like I'm in charge all the time. Now will you show me your submarine?"

It was funny how Tom's mood could change just like that. He wiped his eyes, and right away he was his usual bright, infinitely energetic self again. He ran over to the enormous train car and dragged open a massive, rumbling sliding door.

When Tom said he had a submarine, what had flashed through Kate's head was something pretty modest. Maybe one of those metal balls with a porthole in the side that you lowered on a cable. Or the yellow submarine from "Yellow Submarine."

But this was different. Tom's submarine was as big as a whale, fifty feet long at least, and as gleaming and intricate as a pocket watch. You could see inside it—the whole exterior was clear as glass, though Kate hoped it was made of something a little sturdier than that—and it was stuffed with tubes and wires and machinery and electronics. The hull was studded with spotlights, and in the rear were some excitingly powerful-looking propellers. There was a hatch on top, and two stubby fins stuck out on either side, with more angled thrusters on the ends.

"Oh," Jag said. "Wow."

"Okay," Kate said. "Okay. That is amazing."

"That's even better than a trampoline car," said Wren.

Tom beamed as if he'd personally constructed the submarine himself, by hand.

"What's it like inside?" Kate said.

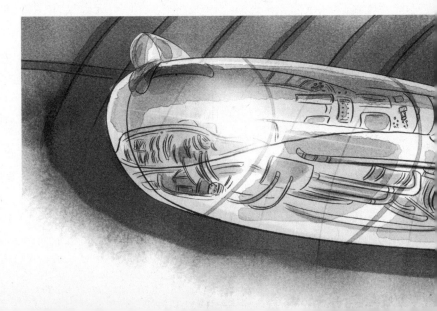

"I don't know!"

It turned out that Tom had had the submarine for all of nine months, ever since his ninth birthday, but he'd never used it, not once. He was afraid that if he showed it to Kate she would take it over and make it hers, but he was also too scared to go in it all by himself. So he'd left it where it was all this time.

"You have to swear a solemn vow," Tom said, "that whatever happens, I am in charge of this submarine."

"I swear," Kate said.

"It's called the *Barracuda*."

"Well, I solemnly swear that the *Barracuda* is your thing. I'm just a passenger."

"You can be a lieutenant if you want. Jag, too. Just

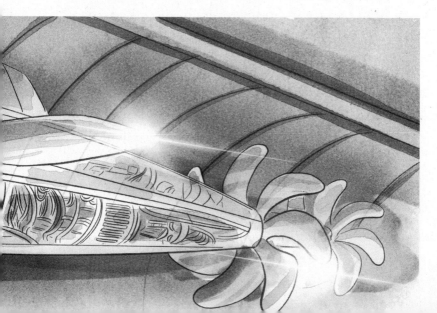

so long as I'm the skipper. And Wren is executive officer."

"Where do you want to go, Skipper Tom?"

"I have no idea!"

But Jag had an idea. He'd obviously been thinking about this for a while. His idea was gray whales.

Gray whales, he explained, lived in the Pacific Ocean. Most of them hung out in the north, off the coast of Alaska, in what was called the Bering Sea. They migrated south to Mexico and back every year, about a ten-thousand-mile round trip. (It was, apparently, the longest migration of any mammal. Though gray whales still had nothing on the swift.)

But there used to be another population of gray whales, an entirely separate one, that lived in the Atlantic Ocean until whalers hunted them to extinction. Gray whales had a reputation as fighters—they rammed and flipped boats when they were attacked, so whalers nicknamed them "devil fish." But it hadn't saved them.

But now it was illegal to hunt gray whales. They were making a comeback in the Pacific. Why not bring them back to the Atlantic, too?

Dive Dive Dive

"OKAY," KATE SAID. "I CAN SEE WHY YOU DIDN'T WANT TO do this by yourself."

The *Silver Arrow* had taken them to the Bering Sea. They weren't far offshore, and the day was calm, but Kate didn't feel calm.

The submarine car had all kinds of machinery in it for deploying the *Barracuda*. When Tom pushed a big red button, it extended a pair of remarkable hydraulic arms out to one side that lowered the submarine with impressive precision into the heaving, tossing ocean, which was as gray as graphite.

It floated there, rising and falling with the passing swells. A jointed gangplank extended automatically and latched on to the submarine's conning tower.

For a minute everybody just watched the submarine and the gangplank go up and down. It was a daunting prospect, one that would've been an opportunity for some bold, steadfast leadership if Kate had felt like providing it. But she didn't. *Not my submarine!*

But then Wren and Tom just looked at each other, nodded, and set off step-by-step along the walkway, staying low and gripping the handrails. When they got to the end, Tom opened the hatch. Wren swung her legs down into it and disappeared into the submarine.

Only then did Kate notice that Jag was looking about as gray as a gray whale.

"What's wrong?"

"I have...fears," he said. "Of drowning."

"I'm not exactly looking forward to it either, but the others are making us look bad. Come on."

Also it was really cold in Alaska in late spring, even in their heavy conductor coats.

Through a pure effort of will, Kate forced herself to totter along the gangplank. The gentle rolling of the ocean felt a lot less gentle when you were rolling with it, and somehow she was overwhelmingly certain that at any moment an orca was going to leap gracefully out of the water, snatch her neatly off the walkway, and disappear with her into the depths, never to be seen again. But Kate decided that was one of those feelings she was not going to indulge.

She felt better once she was inside the *Barracuda*. It was cramped, and she couldn't quite stand upright, but somehow it felt cozy rather than claustrophobic. Tom and Wren had already installed themselves in the pilot and copilot seats, which were a lot cushier than the stools in the cab of the *Silver Arrow*. In front of them was a semicircular console crammed with dials and lights and buttons and joysticks and little video screens that wouldn't have looked out of place in the cockpit of a 747.

Along the top of the console ran a strip of screen with words scrolling along it—apparently that was how the *Barracuda* talked. It was walking Tom and

Wren through the launch procedure on a level of technical detail that would've put the observatory car to shame.

There were two more of the cushy seats toward the rear, for passengers. Or lieutenants, she supposed.

"I'll just take one of these chairs in the back!" she called out to Tom and Wren. They ignored her, but the *Barracuda* answered, on a screen running the length of the hull:

IT'S NOT THE BACK

IT'S THE STERN

"Oh," Kate said. "Right. I guess we are on a ship."

A SUBMARINE IS NOT A SHIP

TECHNICALLY IT'S A BOAT

It was turning out that the *Barracuda* was a serious soul. It never joked. It could leave the sarcasm to those carefree vehicles that roamed the surface world. Undersea travel was serious business. Still, its seats were leather and generously padded.

Jag made his way back to join her in a terrified half walk, half crawl. He climbed into the other seat and pulled up his gangly legs and hugged them.

"You look a little freaked out," Kate said.

"Because I am an air-breathing animal! This is not my natural environment!"

Kate herself was getting less and less freaked out. The *Barracuda*'s serious attitude was reassuring. From below, through the submarine's transparent sides, the water looked more of an inviting milky blue-green than a sinister gray.

"Closing hatch!" Tom called out.

"Releasing davits!" Wren answered.

"Starting ventilation!"

Then together: "Dive dive dive!"

The *Barracuda* dove.

Hordes of bubbles burbled violently up from tanks on either side of the hull, and spray washed up its glassy sides—it was a bit like being in one of those car washes where you get to ride inside the car. The surface of the sea rose up and away and closed over their heads. As they sank the light got dimmer, and gradually all the colors washed out of everything, all except the grays and blues. Sounds became hushed, except for the soft clicking and beeping of the *Barracuda*'s various internal functions. Funny things happened inside Kate's inner ears.

Tom and Wren wrestled with the controls, getting them level in the water, forward and aft and port and starboard. It was all very high-tech compared with the steam trains, but Kate supposed that if she was going to be plunged a hundred feet under the ocean, she would probably want to do it in a vessel a little more modern than 1938. She felt rather than heard the rear thrusters fire up; they ran on electric power and were virtually noiseless. The *Barracuda* moved so smoothly that Kate was only occasionally reminded that they were moving at all, when they passed little scraps of floating marine stuff and tiny stray silver bubbles. Very occasionally a few fish would fade into view from out of the depths, then vanish again with a twitch of their tails.

It came as a surprise when the pale sandy ocean floor loomed up underneath them like the surface of the moon. Something gray and sinuous squiggled away in a cloud of sediment. Jag's eyes were flicking around the submarine as if he were looking for an emergency exit or an escape pod or maybe an inter-dimensional portal.

Kate tried to take his mind off it.

"So," she said quietly. "I heard you used to be homeschooled."

He paused for a second, blinking, before he answered. "That's right. For a long time my mother worked and my father taught me. It was a good arrangement. I think he always wanted to be a professor."

"So how come you stopped?"

Jag frowned.

"I guess I was starting to feel like my dad was my only friend. I'm an only child, and he's my connection to the railroad too—he's my 'Uncle Herbert.' It's a lot, and it was all great, but I guess I just needed something more...normal. Like friends my own age. I mean, Wren's great—her mother works with my mom, that's how we found her—but it's not the same. My dad was really angry when I told him. Still is, I guess."

He studied his fingernails. "The irony is that now I'm in regular school and I still don't have any friends."

Kate kicked his foot lightly. "We're friends," she said.

"I mean at school."

Kate wanted to say that they were friends at school, too, but she knew it wasn't true. She never talked to him at school, at least not in front of other people. She suddenly got very interested in her own fingernails.

"I wonder how we find the whales," she said.

"The *Barracuda* knows," Wren said.

I'LL CALL THEM

A series of loud, deep, resonant *pop*s echoed through the boat. Apparently, that was how gray whales talked to each other.

"Can't they talk like the other animals?" Kate asked. "I mean, so we can understand?"

THEY COULD

THEY JUST DON'T WANT TO

For a long time after that nothing happened. They traveled in silence, cruising along with ghostly serenity ten feet above the smooth ocean floor. Moisture beaded on the curved inside of the hull.

"There used to be a lot more kelp in the Bering Sea," Jag said after a while. "But because of climate change, the water's getting warmer and the plankton are dying off. That and overfishing are killing off the fish, which is bad because that's what the sea lions eat. Killer whales feed on sea lions, so with fewer sea lions around now, the killer whales are having to prey on sea otters instead."

"Okay," Kate said. But Jag was just getting warmed up.

"Sea otters eat sea urchins, and with a lot of the sea otters gone, the sea urchin population is exploding. The sea urchins are what's eating up all the kelp, which means—"

"Okay! Jag! Can I please just look at the water for a little while without feeling bad?!"

Jag went quiet and hugged his knees again. They almost didn't notice when the whale arrived.

She matched course with the *Barracuda* gracefully and effortlessly. First she wasn't there, and then she was. It was hard to believe that something so huge could be so gentle. She was dark gray but mottled all over with a curious tracery of pale gray barnacles—she looked like a chalkboard that had been scribbled on and then partly erased, or a map of the dark side of the moon. Her mouth was a long, thoughtful upside-down smile that ran right to the corner of her eye.

With the *Barracuda* acting as translator, Jag explained his idea to them. Paradoxically, it would rely on global warming to work: Temperatures in the Arctic were so high now in the summertime that the sea ice was clear all the way along the northern coast of Canada. Theoretically a pod of gray whales could swim north out of the Bering Sea, then east following the coastline, through the Arctic Ocean and then south again all the way down into the North Atlantic. There they could establish a new colony, ranging up and down the Eastern Seaboard, from Nova Scotia down to the warm seas off Florida, in waters where gray whales had lived for thousands of years.

More grays loomed up out of the darkness and joined them, and the conversation popped and boomed back and forth between them, and with more distant pods, too—sound carried for miles underwater. When it was over, a small pod of whales had agreed to make the journey.

That was when the *Barracuda* really came into its own. It led the pod of adventurous whales, keeping pace with them, imitating their movements, almost becoming one of them. It couldn't match them for agility—they looked all grave and solemn, but they loved to leap up out of the water and crash back into it and smack their massive tails on the surface, just for fun. But the *Barracuda* was every bit as quick, and it made itself useful when the whales were attacked by orcas, which were their only predator—its hull was impervious to their teeth, and it turned out to have a couple of torpedo tubes hidden away with all its other equipment. By the time Kate and the others reached the Labrador Sea, off the coast of Greenland, they'd almost forgotten they weren't sea-dwelling mammals themselves.

That was when a call came through from the *Golden Swift*. They had to come home, right away. The railway had delivered a new timetable, and it had only one stop on it. That stop was:

ACHNASHELLACH

Oh No

THE FIRST TIME THEY'D COME TO ACHNASHELLACH IT had been at sundown, and it was sundown this time, too. The country was rough as ever, with rugged-looking mountains and swaths of treeless scrub breaking up the pine forests. The orange sun flickered between thin trunks.

But it didn't feel the same. Last time Kate was here she'd been Detective Kate, looking for clues. This time she thought she knew what they'd find. Jag had released the lynx and set the forest back on the course to balance.

But if that were true, then they wouldn't be here. The Great Secret Intercontinental Railway didn't send them where there weren't any problems.

Kate and Jag climbed out at the station together warily. The platform was long and empty and littered with fallen pine cones. She had to scan it twice before she noticed that anybody was there at all.

It was a single lynx. He was lying at the very far end of the platform in a patch of shadow. His golden eyes glowed in the twilight, and he was panting rapidly, even though the day was cool.

Kate approached cautiously.

"I'm from the railroad," she said. "Do you need help?"

The lynx turned as if he'd just noticed her, and Jag, and the train for the first time.

"I'm all right," he said.

But up close he didn't look all right. His silvery dappled coat was dirty and twisted and matted with blood in places. He was too thin, and one of his magnificent tufted ears was missing its tip.

"What happened here?"

"Bit of trouble."

A spot of bother, the cassowary would've said. The lynx bent his head to lick at a dark patch in his fur.

"Where are the others?" Jag said.

"Not coming."

Kate's heart was sinking. Something had gone wrong here. She glanced at Jag, and there was a fear in his eyes she'd never seen before. She heard the rough scratch of claws on cement: It was the wolverine. Ignoring her, he went right up to the lynx and sniffed him.

"He's half starved," the wolverine announced. "And he's been shot in the leg—the bone's broken. It's all right," he said to the lynx, and his voice had a gentle note in it that he never used with humans. "We're going to help you."

Kate ran to the caboose, where there was a chest of medical supplies, while the others helped the lynx onto a blanket, which they used as a makeshift stretcher. They took him to Jag's sleeper car and put him on the bed. The bullet had broken the lynx's leg but then gone out the other side, so they didn't have to dig it out. They splinted the leg and disinfected and patched his wounds. He had a couple of cracked ribs, too, which they taped as best they could, though they had to shave some of the lynx's beautiful fur to do it.

Through all this the lynx never complained, though he growled and hissed in the bad moments. Piece by piece they got the story out of him.

The three other lynx from the *Golden Swift* were all dead.

"It started out fine," the big cat said. "Just like we talked about. Plenty of deer. Plenty of fox. Plenty of forest—we lynx like to spread out, have our own territories to ourselves. It was perfect." He took a breath and then winced at his ribs. "But there was a flock of sheep grazing in the hills, and one day we couldn't resist having a look. Didn't take any, just gave them a sniff, but a farmer must've seen us, because pretty soon there was a hunting party out searching the woods. They had guns. And dogs. They killed two of us. The third ran onto a highway and a car hit him.

"I was lucky. They shot me, but only in the leg, and I hid till they stopped looking. Haven't eaten in a week." He turned his lamplike eyes on Jag. "It wasn't how we thought it was going to be."

"I'm sorry," Jag said.

He was in shock. All Kate could think about was how brave animals were. The lynx didn't pity himself, and he didn't sit around wishing he hadn't come, or raging at Jag for bringing him there. He was just looking for a way forward.

"I'm so sorry." Tears were running down Jag's cheeks now, but his voice was steady. "It wasn't supposed to be like that."

The lynx didn't answer, just gave his splint a sniff and a shake, then put his head on his paws and closed his eyes. They left him to rest.

The *Golden Swift* was moving again, heading back to Siberia to take the last lynx home.

"How could I have been so stupid?" Jag looked grim as they walked forward toward the engine. "I should've known it wouldn't work. I should've known it wasn't that simple."

Kate had never seen Jag anything other than one hundred percent confident. He was always so sure of himself. She knew what it was to be wrong; she expected to make mistakes. But she suspected that he wasn't so used to it.

"The theory wasn't wrong," she said. "I guess people just weren't ready for it. They didn't understand."

"People are horrible," Jag said bitterly.

They stopped in the dining car and sat, but neither of them was hungry. They were both reeling inside. Kate realized she'd learned the wrong lesson from the Demilitarized Zone. The lesson was that they should've left nature alone. Instead they'd tried to fix it and just made it worse.

Kate wished Uncle Herbert were here. He would've known what to say.

"Maybe we should've reached out to them beforehand," she said. "Talked to them. Gotten them ready."

"How?!" Jag was in a fog of frustration and horror. "What would we say? I was so stupid to think

I could fix anything! The wolverine was right all along."

"We have to go back," Kate said.

"I know."

"To the other places where we brought back animals, to make sure things like this didn't happen there too."

"I know!"

They were silent again, thinking terrible thoughts. What if the other animals—the otters and tortoises and kestrels and the Père David's deer—had run into the same kind of trouble? What if all this time, while they told themselves they were fixing everything, they'd just been sowing disaster and destruction wherever they went?

The wolverine arrived carrying a haunch of raw meat in his toothy jaws. Nothing wrong with his appetite. He glared at them.

"We know," Jag said glumly. "You don't have to say it."

The wolverine began to devour his haunch messily, crunching bone.

"I know you tried," he said.

That wasn't what Kate was expecting.

"I know you thought you were doing good," the wolverine growled. "In your own pathetic, miserable, stupid human way."

A phone rang. It was one of the old-fashioned phones on the wall that Jag used to talk to the *Golden Swift*. He picked it up and listened, then held it out to Kate.

"It's for you."

That was odd. She put it to her ear, and that same musical, crystal-chiming voice spoke.

"*Did you know,*" it said, "*that in the old days people believed that swifts never landed at all? They thought they didn't have feet, only wings.*"

"I...did not know that. They do actually have feet, right?"

"*Yes. They can fly a thousand miles in one go, but even swifts have to land.*"

"I guess people used to be pretty bad at science." Kate wasn't in a bantering mood. "Why are you telling me this now?"

"*Because I know you want to keep flying,*" the crystal voice said. "*I know you wish you could fly forever. But everybody has to land sometime. And I think it's about to happen to you.*"

Kate frowned at the receiver.

"What do you mean?"

There was no answer.

"I think we're slowing down," Jag said.

"We can't be there already."

"Never underestimate the *Swift*."

But something was off. Kate slid open a window and leaned out to see what was up ahead.

"I could be completely wrong about this," she said, "but it looks like there's an elephant on the tracks."

The Fall of the *Golden Swift*

KATE HAD MET ELEPHANTS BEFORE—A COUPLE OF them, anyway. In her experience they were generally good-humored and tremendously dignified and appropriately apologetic about the fact that their incredible size made them really hard to transport. (They could, with a lot of patience and effort on all sides, be stuffed into a boxcar.)

But this elephant didn't want to be transported. She stood on the tracks as immovable as a landslide, staring down the *Golden Swift*.

"Stop," she said.

"It's all right," Kate said. "We've stopped."

"You've stopped the train," the elephant said. "Now we want you to stop it all."

Kate wasn't even sure where in the world they were. They were surrounded by a thin forest of shaggy-barked trees rooted in dusty red earth. The elephant wasn't alone, there was a whole crowd of animals behind her on the track: monkeys and birds and lizards and dogs and big cats all mixed together, still and silent, watching her. There were more elephants, too, a whole herd of them.

"We've got an injured lynx on board," Jag said. "We need to get him back to Siberia."

"We know what you're doing. We've been watching you." This wasn't the elephant, it was a black bird that was sitting on top of the elephant's head. "Moving animals around, putting them where you think they should go. You think you're helping, but you're only making things worse. We want you to stop it."

"I'm sorry," Jag said. "It was my idea, nobody else's."

"We don't care. We just want you to leave us alone."

"But we're on your side!" Kate said.

You have no idea how hard it is to argue with an elephant until you've actually tried it. They're so firm, so calm, so determined, so large—it's like trying to argue with a boulder.

"Haven't you figured it out by now? Humans can only be on their own side. We haven't just come to stop you personally, we're shutting down the whole Great Secret Intercontinental Railway. For good."

"What? But you can't!"

"Yes," the elephant said. "We can."

This was too much. Kate had helped animals. Whatever mistakes she'd made, she'd helped the fishing cat and the baby pangolin, the mamba and the heron, and hundreds and hundreds more. She'd even helped the wolverine. She knew she had!

They were interrupted by the sound of the *Golden Swift*'s whistle: five short sharp blasts. It was an emergency signal.

While they'd been talking, the elephants and the other big beasts had formed a line and placed their foreheads against the *Golden Swift*. Now they pushed. For a second Kate wasn't worried—there was no way even a bunch of elephants could push over a steam train! But then they all took a step forward together and the *Golden Swift* tilted up sideways onto one set of wheels.

"Stop!"

Tom and Wren were running along the tracks. They must've raided the dojo car, because Tom had his nunchucks at the ready, and Wren had a wooden staff almost as long as she was. Behind them came the cassowary, looking as dangerous as she ever had, with the wolverine following closely. For once Kate was grateful for his terrifying wildness.

"What are you doing?" the bird said from on top of the elephant. "You hate humans!"

"Of course I do!" the wolverine snarled back. He

was obviously struggling with himself. "Just...not these ones!"

"Children," the elephant said. "Please."

Two more elephants stepped forward, and Kate saw uncertainty flicker over Tom's face. He started to back away. But the elephants weren't uncertain: one picked up Tom with his trunk, and the other picked up Wren, and they simply placed them, dazed but unharmed, on their backs.

Kate knew they never would've hit an animal anyway.

The cassowary and the wolverine knew when they were beaten. All they could do was watch as the elephants gave the *Golden Swift* another shove. It tilted farther, and balanced for a long, agonizing second.

"Stop!" Jag had never once yelled at the bullies who taunted him, but now he shouted at the animals at the top of his lungs. "Stop what you're doing! Please!"

But they didn't stop. With a scream of its whistle the *Swift* tipped over, off the tracks, tearing free of the coal tender behind it, and smashed down onto its side with an impact that shook the earth.

Metal groaned and protested, and every piece of

glass in the train shattered and sprayed onto the red dirt. Steam leaked out of little rips in the metal.

At least the boiler didn't explode, Kate thought numbly. An image flashed through her head of a train she and Tom had seen once, the *Twilight Star*, that had been left standing broken and gutted and rusted out all by itself in an empty field. She didn't think she could stand it if the *Golden Swift* ended up that way. Jag watched, frozen, with one hand held out as if he could somehow stop what was happening.

But it had already happened. He crouched down with his hands over his head to shut out the disaster.

Kate put a hand on his shaking shoulder. She'd wrecked the *Silver Arrow* once, when it fell through the ice into a frozen lake. But from there it had fallen into the Roundhouse, where trains went to be repaired. It was hard to see how the *Golden Swift* was going to get to the Roundhouse from here. She didn't understand how the animals could've done it. She heard in her head the *Swift*'s lovely crystal voice on its old-fashioned telephone. How could they be so cruel? Except then she thought about how many times poachers had killed elephants just for the ivory in their tusks. And she thought of those three lynx dead in Scotland. What wouldn't she do if someone did something like that to the people she loved?

A warm breeze blew, carrying a faint sweet honey smell from the trees. They looked familiar— eucalyptus, that's what they were. The kind koalas ate. They must be in Australia.

"Kate!"

A familiar figure in a yellow blazer was pushing through the crowd of animals to get to her.

"Uncle Herbert!"

Kate was so relieved to see him that she flung her arms around his neck. At least there was this: Silly old Uncle Herbert was alive and well!

"We looked everywhere for you! I was so worried!"

"I knew you must have been," Uncle Herbert said. "But I was perfectly all right."

Though when she let go of him, Kate could see that he'd been better. His yellow suit was dusty and torn, and what there was of his hair was long and lank.

"But what happened to you?!"

"The animals kidnapped me. A lion and a tiger came to my house in the middle of the night. Lions and tigers hardly ever agree on anything, so when they do, you know there's not much point in resisting.

"They've taken perfectly good care of me. Though the food's awful, and I've been very bored. I taught some monkeys to play hearts, but they only ever try to shoot the moon."

"A wolverine pooed in your hot tub."

He sighed philosophically. "These things happen." Though Kate wasn't convinced that things like that did happen, generally speaking.

"Why did they kidnap you?"

"They want to shut down the railroad," Uncle Herbert said. "Did they tell you? I keep trying to explain that they've vastly overestimated my importance in the scheme of things, but they won't listen. I see you found Jag."

"Was that— You knew about him?"

"That's why I left you the note about Achnashellach. We junior agents aren't as dumb as we look, you know. People almost never are."

"But do you think it's true what the animals are saying?" Kate took a deep breath. "I mean—could they really be better off without us?"

Before he could answer, the air was filled by the loudest sound Kate had ever heard. It was a train whistle, but it came from everywhere at once. It was so loud the leaves on the trees rattled and the dust on the ground shook. Everybody looked around for what could've made it.

Approaching through the trees was a very strange sight: a train where there shouldn't have been one. Or not a train, just a single train car. A plain, ordinary flat car. No engine pulled it, it moved all by itself, and it ran on tracks that simply rose out of the ground ahead of it. They shone bright in the sun like they were made of pure gold.

Everyone fell silent. There wouldn't have been much doubt about who it was even if there hadn't been a sign on the side of the car.

The sign read:

THE BOARD OF DIRECTORS

It's About Time

NO ONE SPOKE AS THE CAR ROLLED SILENTLY UP TO where Kate and the others stood. It carried the strangest collection of creatures Kate had ever seen, and that was saying something.

There was a tremendous brown tortoise. There was also a large crested green lizard—sitting on top of the tortoise—and an ominous-looking bird with massive black wings, a completely bald black head, and a downy white ruff around its neck that made it look a bit like Cruella de Vil. The bird was perched on a branch of a short, squat, incredibly gnarled pine tree that was so old it seemed to have given up growing upward and taken up growing sideways instead and gotten fatter and fatter till its bark had split.

Also on the Board of Directors' car was an apparently empty tank of water. The car glided noiselessly to a stop on its golden rails. Everybody stared.

"I told you we'd be late," the tortoise said to his companions. "But you wanted to make a dramatic entrance. And now look what's happened!"

"Conductors Kate, Tom, Jag, and Wren," the lizard said, ignoring the tortoise, "it's a pleasure to meet you after all this time. And Junior Agent Yastremzski, of course."

Uncle Herbert did his best to straighten his torn and dusty blazer.

"We, as you've no doubt guessed, are the Board of Directors of the Great Secret Intercontinental Railway," the bird said. "Our members are drawn from among the oldest creatures on the planet. I am an Andean condor, I'm seventy-seven years old, and I'm the youngest member of the board. This reptile"—he inclined his head toward the lizard—"is a tuatara. He's a hundred and four. He may appear to be a lizard, but in fact tuataras belong to their own taxonomic order, the rhynchocephalians."

"Also I have three eyes," said the tuatara. "Fact."

"It's not a fact," the tortoise said irritably. "He loves to brag about it, but the third eye is vestigial. Tuataras only see out of it as hatchlings, and even then it's only light and dark."

"Until *you* can see light and dark out of your forehead, my friend," the tuatara said mildly, "I don't see where you're in any position to pass judgment."

The tortoise rolled her eyes.

"I am an Aldabra tortoise," she said. "I am two hundred and twelve. Yesterday was my birthday."

"Happy birthday," Kate said automatically.

"Thank you."

An awkward pause followed.

"I apologize," the condor said. "I don't think any of you can hear the jellyfish. Or the pine tree."

"Nuts," said the tuatara. "The magics must not extend that far."

"Well, that tank of water"—the tortoise nodded at it with her ancient brown head—"contains a single specimen of *Turritopsis dohrnii*, the so-called immortal jellyfish. He—" The tortoise stopped for a second as if she'd been silently interrupted. "That's what I said. Immortal jellyfish. He claims to be—" Another interruption. The tortoise rolled her eyes again. "I'm not going to repeat what the jellyfish said, but *according to him* he is nine hundred and twenty-six years old."

"Theoretically, *Turritopsis dohrnii* can live forever," the tuatara explained. "When they're threatened, they have the ability to turn themselves back into babies. Then they grow up again. They can do it as many times as they want. He's very tiny, only about a quarter inch across, so you probably can't see him."

"And this tree on which I am sitting," the condor

said, "is a Great Basin bristlecone pine. Like most pine trees, they are both male and female, so we refer to them as *they*. They are about four thousand years old—they're not very precise about time. To put that number in perspective, this tree was a sapling around the time Stonehenge was being built. The ancient Egyptians were just inventing hieroglyphics. This tree witnessed the births of Judaism, Christianity, and Islam and the reigns of all twenty-four kings of Israel and five hundred and fifty-nine emperors of China. They have outlived the Greek, Roman, British, Japanese, Abbasid, and Mongol empires. Yes?"

Tom's hand was raised.

"You have a bird, a plant, a jellyfish, and two reptiles. Why aren't there any mammals on the board?"

"Very good question. The oldest mammals are bowhead whales. They can live for well over two hundred years. We consult them occasionally, but for obvious reasons it's not very practical for them to attend meetings. The longest-lived mammals on land are human beings. Human beings aren't invited to join the Board of Directors, also for obvious reasons.

"Now." The condor turned to the elephant. "Why are you destroying one of our trains?"

"Why would you build a train in the first place?" the elephant shot back.

"Animal magic is powerful," the condor said. "Animal sorcerers are much more powerful than human ones, though you wouldn't know that from books. But humans have created new kinds of problems, which our magics were never meant to solve. To address them we have been forced to use forms of human technology."

"And why would you trust humans with them?!"

"Many humans want to solve Earth's problems."

"Yes, and they're just making everything worse!" Kate had never heard an elephant trying not to lose her temper, but she was pretty sure that's what this one was doing. "You can't fix nature if you don't understand it. It has to stop! You've seen what happens in places where humans don't go. Could it be any clearer? Nature just wants to be left alone!"

If the condor was intimidated by this speech, he didn't show it.

"But aren't humans part of nature?"

"No," the elephant's bird said crisply. "They have disqualified themselves. They have made war on nature. Therefore they are not part of nature."

"Really?" the tortoise said. "And that's for you to decide, is it? Would you prefer the world back the way it was before humans arrived?"

"Yes!"

This wasn't just the elephant. Most of the animals said it together.

"But what exactly does that mean?" asked the tuatara.

There was a faint creaking sound, and the pine tree's ancient branches stirred as if in a breeze, but there was no breeze. The world all around them changed: The ground shook under their feet like in an earthquake, and the trees vibrated in place till they blurred.

The tree had cast a spell. It all happened in a couple of seconds, and when it was over, they were no longer in a forest.

"The tree has transported us," the condor said. "But not in space. We have gone back in time to the Pleistocene epoch. This is Australia fifty thousand years ago."

The woods were mostly gone. In their place, dry grasslands stretched out in all directions, broken by clumps of trees. (They still looked more or less like eucalyptus.) Not far off was a clump of huge beasts

about the size and shape of hippos, but covered in thick brown fur, and with muzzles and black noses like bears. A few of them tore leaves off a bush while others scanned the horizon for predators.

Farther away stood a pair of dun-colored birds, each one easily eight feet tall. Their heads were massive, like ax-heads perched on their skinny necks, and matched by bare legs so muscular they looked like they belonged to rugby players. They put the cassowary's legs to shame.

"The big wombats over there are diprotodons,"

the tuatara said, indicating the hairy hippos. "They're the largest marsupials that ever lived. Majestic, aren't they?"

"You wouldn't want one to corner you at a party, though," the tortoise said dryly. "Not very bright."

"And the big birds are dromornithids," the tuatara went on. "They're one of the largest birds that ever lived. I suppose things were just bigger back then—somewhere around here there are some Megalania, which are the biggest lizards that ever lived. There were giant kangaroos, too, and a six-foot horned tortoise. And no"—Tom's hand was up—"they're not dinosaurs. Humans think everything was dinosaurs!"

"Everything *should* be dinosaurs," Tom muttered.

"They died out sixty million years ago!" the tortoise snapped. "Get over it!"

"The point is," the condor explained, "this is Australia at the very moment before the first humans got here. They'll be arriving any minute now, island-hopping from New Guinea in open boats. Everything was different. Right now in North America there are camels and giant ground sloths and dire wolves. Europe has rhinos and scimitar cats and the Irish elk, whose antlers were twelve feet across."

"This is exactly what I'm talking about!" the elephant said indignantly. "You think it's a coincidence that none of those animals are around anymore? Wherever humans go, animals go extinct!"

"But what we're talking about," the condor said patiently, "is the world we live in now. You want to put things back the way they were, but what is the way they were? How far back do you want to go? You wouldn't recognize the world before humans got here. You can't separate them from nature. They're too much a part of it.

"You might not like it—even *you* might not like it, Kate and Jag—but it's too late to go back."

We Meet Again

"WELL, LET'S GO FORWARD, THEN!" THE ELEPHANT SAID. "Without humans! And without your ridiculous railroad either!"

The condor leaned his head close to the glass tank for a few seconds.

"The jellyfish asks how you plan to do that. Are you going to make humanity extinct?"

"We could," the elephant said grimly. "Humans are vulnerable to disease, especially ones they catch from animals. Anthrax, Ebola, smallpox, bubonic plague, leprosy—they all came from animals. We're pretty sure they caught COVID-19 from a bat."

"If you destroy humanity," the tuatara said, "you'll be no better than humanity."

"Nonsense. Humans aren't animals, they're a disease themselves. Tell me, humans: What happens when you meet a wild animal in a field or a forest? What does that animal do?"

"It runs away," Jag said glumly.

"The first lesson any wild animal learns from birth is to run when they see a human coming. Imagine that. There is no more terrible monster."

"I have a question," Kate said.

The elephant turned its huge, deep eyes on her. The directors looked at her, too, or at least the ones with eyes did.

"I want to call a witness," she said. "I want to ask the fishing cat a question."

The Board of Directors gathered around the tank of the immortal jellyfish again and conferred quietly. It could only have been a minute or so, but when you know people are talking about you, a minute seems to last about seven years.

Finally they returned to their places. The pine tree waved its branches again. This time nothing happened, or nothing seemed to happen—but then, looking around curiously, blinking at the light, the fishing cat came padding out from behind the tree.

It was just so good to see her, with her funny sleek head and her olive fur and her big black stripes and her thick, heavy tail, that for a second Kate forgot why she was here. She forgot everything and just went running to her, tears flowing down her face. When the fishing cat saw her she leaped into Kate's arms, and since she weighed about twenty pounds Kate promptly fell down backward in the fifty-thousand-year-old grass, hugging her old friend and crying into the soft fur of her neck.

"I missed you," Kate whispered. "I missed you so much!"

The fishing cat put a paw on each of her shoulders and looked down at her face with serious golden eyes. She smelled faintly of fish.

"Everything's gone so wrong!" Kate said.

"I thought it must have, if the Board of Directors wanted to see me. Is it worse than last time?"

"I don't know! Maybe!"

"Because last time was pretty bad," the fishing cat said.

"This time is, too. It's so bad!"

"It looks like a train fell over."

"I know!"

"Remember when we almost fell off a cliff?"

"I remember that." Kate wiped her eyes. "And when we turned into trees?"

"I remember," the fishing cat said. "I remember spring."

"I hate to interrupt," the elephant said coldly, "but what is the point of all this?"

Reluctantly Kate set the cat aside and got to her feet.

"Listening to you talk," she said, "I can't help wondering if you're right. Maybe we are as bad as you think we are. And I remember that the last time I felt like this, the fishing cat and my other animal friends helped. They saw something in me that I couldn't see in myself, something that wasn't all bad. If only I could remember what it was."

Now out from behind the Great Basin bristlecone pine slithered the familiar bright green stripe of the mamba. The porcupine waddled out next, and then the little pangolin—all grown up now, a full three feet long and impressively scaly. Even the polar bear came. She'd obviously found more food at the North Pole, because she was back at her fighting weight, and very imposing she was, too.

The mamba appointed himself the spokesman, or spokescreature, and slithered smoothly up the bristlecone pine to address the crowd.

"I understand how upsssssset you all are," he hissed. "But as a venomous creature, I can also understand what it is to be feared the way humans are feared.

"The thing you have to understand about humans is that they aren't like us, in bad ways but also good ones. It's something about those big swollen brains of theirs. It makes them different, and not just from us but from each other. Some are bad, but some are good. It's like each human being is its own species. If you got rid of them, it would be like making seven billion species extinct all at once."

In her heart Kate clutched at this idea. Maybe it was possible. Maybe she could be one of the good ones.

"But aren't we missing someone?" The tortoise seemed to be going over a mental list. "Wasn't there one more animal on the *Silver Arrow*? A bird—a white-bellied heron, I believe?"

The snake, the cat, the porcupine, the pangolin, and the bear all looked at one another and then, all together, at the silent squat figure of the ancient bristlecone pine. But no heron strode out from behind it. Instead the tree just twisted their trunk very slightly, back and forth, left and right.

There was no mistaking what the tree meant. There was no heron anymore. The last time she saw the white-bellied heron, the *Silver Arrow* was taking her to a new home where Kate thought she'd be safe. But the heron hadn't been safe there. Something had happened, and she was gone.

It was too much. Kate put her face in her hands and sobbed.

She didn't just sob; she howled. She howled and howled. Tom was crying, too, and they hugged each other desperately. Kate never knew she could feel so

much sadness. A hole had opened up inside her so deep and so wide she felt like she would never climb out of it again.

And in a way it was true. She would feel happiness again one day, maybe even one day soon, but something in her had changed. A shadow had fallen over her that would never lift all the way. She would never be exactly the same as she was before.

But at the same time something was tugging at the back of her mind, something else in the here and now. There had been a warm wind before, but now it was hot, and it carried a sharp smell with it. Smoke.

It was a bushfire. A wall of smoke was visible above the trees, a dark veil rising into the sky. It was far away, almost on the horizon, but she knew enough about forest fires to know that they moved fast. There was no time to grieve. It was time to go. Somehow she pushed her sorrow down somewhere out of the way, and, making no apologies, she scrambled up onto the Board of Directors' flat car.

"Listen, everybody!"

A sea of animal faces looked up at her, big and small, furry and scaly, muzzled and beaked.

"I know the last thing you want to do right now is listen to a human! But there are some problems only humans can solve, and this is one of them! If you want to live, you're going to have to do exactly what I say!"

The poor *Golden Swift* lay in the red dust like a beached whale, shattered glass all around it, a ruin of its former gleaming glory. Shouting, cajoling, ordering, begging, Kate got the biggest animals lined up with their heads and shoulders against the roof of the fallen engine, and together they shoved it, grinding and scraping over dirt and stones, back toward the tracks.

The air was filling with ash, and the hot wind was almost choking. Red veins of fire were twisting up among the farthest trees. Kate could hear it now, a huge, deep roaring and crackling as the hungry flames fed on the forest. More animals were pouring out of the woods ahead of them: bounding kangaroos and wallabies, silly waddling echidnas, and innumerable little mousy and squirrelly creatures. Numbats maybe, Kate thought. Or dunnarts.

Straining, lowing, snarling, and roaring, the animals heaved at the *Golden Swift* till it tilted up past the tipping point, wavered there for a second, and then slammed mightily down onto the tracks. It crashed down so hard that it nearly tipped over the other way, and it shed a few more battered golden panels from its aerodynamic trim.

But it was upright again. Jag and Wren clambered into the cab to start setting things right. Kate followed, slowly, so limp with sadness and exhaustion that she hardly knew who or where she was. She just hoped all the animals would fit.

The Garden Car

CHARGING THROUGH WILDFIRES IN THE *GOLDEN SWIFT* was as close to a trip through hell as Kate hoped she would ever take. Day changed to night as smoke blotted out the sun and the sky. The whole world was blackened, and the only light was the orange glow of burning trees and the jets and scraps and whorls of hungry fire all around them. There were pools of it on the ground, and whole bushes and trees were outlined in orange flame. Fire crawled up tree trunks like an army of ants. The air was full of drifting sparks and embers.

Tom drove while Kate and Jag and Wren managed

the animals, who were crammed into every available crevice of the train, from the passenger cars to the caboose. No one spoke, they all just sat there glumly staring out at the disaster all around them, breathing the hot, smoky air, which barely had enough oxygen in it, and thinking about their narrow escape.

Kate wondered if the Board of Directors had set it all up to happen that way—if the board had put them in the path of a fire on purpose to try to teach them all a lesson. She understood now, really understood, what the bristlecone pine had been trying to show them when it took them back in time. It was too late to get rid of humans. Nature had created them, but then humans had gotten too powerful, and now nature was stuck with them. If humans couldn't learn to respect nature they would destroy it, and themselves with it. But if animals and humans were going to survive, they would have to figure out how to do it together. There was no other way.

Whatever the consequences. And the consequences of the consequences.

Kate supposed that in a way she'd saved the day—she was the hero for once, not the villain—but her sense of triumph was already fading. All she could think about was the poor lost heron. *Maybe I could've saved her,* she thought bitterly. *If those animals hadn't kidnapped Uncle Herbert, maybe I could've gone in the* Silver Arrow *and gotten her and taken her somewhere safer.*

But she would never know. She could never know what might have happened. And even if it was true, even if she could've saved the heron, it was still probably humans who killed her, one way or another, with a bullet or fossil fuels or a parking lot or a hydro-electric dam. The trail always led back to humans in the end.

The bushfires seemed like they would go on forever, but of course they didn't. Even something as terrible as that had to end sometime. Soon the magic of the Great Secret Intercontinental Railway whisked them far away, to a mountain pass somewhere in the Alps. It was strange to suddenly be somewhere that wasn't burning, where the air was cold and fresh and the sun was out and the sky was blue. Kate's hair and clothes were still full of smoke. It felt like it would never come out.

There was still a lot of work to do, hundreds of animals to find homes for. It would take days. They decided, all four of the Arrows and the Swifts, that they wanted to do it together. With Uncle Herbert's help they would take the *Golden Swift* to the Roundhouse, and then Kate and Tom and Jag and Wren would work in shifts on the *Silver Arrow*.

When it was Jag and Wren's turn to drive, Kate went back to her Slumberliner and took a long bath and changed clothes and lay down on the bed. It wasn't as restful as it might have been, since her sleeper car was crammed full of animal refugees. She was just about drifting off to sleep when something crawly touched her hand and she practically startled out of her skin.

It was in fact the worst thing possible, a gigantic bug—but she recognized it. It wasn't just any bug. It was an American burying beetle.

Still trying to slow her racing heart, she put her ear close to the huge insect.

"We heard about what happened to the lynx."
Kate could just barely make out what the beetle was
saying. "We felt very sad."

"I did, too."

"We like lynx. They kill lots of small animals for
us to bury."

"I hadn't thought about it that way," Kate said.
"But I guess they probably do."

"But what we wanted to tell you is that even
though it didn't work with the lynx, it worked with
us. We're all alive and safe and happy on our island.
You really helped us."

"I'm glad."

Kate was starting to cry again.

"We have little babies now."

"Oh, good."

"They're eating the pigeon corpses."

"As they should."

His message delivered, the beetle crawled off again to somewhere safer.

Still Kate couldn't sleep. She kept thinking about something the elephant had said. It had bothered her at the time, and it still bothered her.

Finally she gave up on sleep, got up, and walked back past the library car and the boxcars and the candy car. For the most part the animals weren't interested in the candy, but a couple of bears were making absolute pigs of themselves. (Really that was unfair to the pigs, who were showing a lot more restraint.) Kate stopped when she got to the car that she swore she would never ever go into again.

It was true what the elephant had said, that wild animals were terrified of humans. It was such a fact of life that Kate had never even really thought about it. And if animals were truly stuck with humans on this planet, then Kate wanted to know what that was like. She wanted to feel that fear. She wanted to feel what the animals felt. She unlatched the door.

Here we go. Yet another terrible, terrible thing her conscience was going to make her do.

The glass was smudged and sooty outside, but inside the garden car was still lush and fresh and green. She breathed in its rich smell, hoping it would calm her a little. The bees were still buzzing away, busy as ever. All the hairs on Kate's arms stood up straight, and her pulse quickened. She wondered what the bees thought of all the drama going on in the outside world. Maybe they hadn't noticed, safe as they were in their little green glass bubble.

She clicked the door closed behind her.

"Hi." Her voice was hoarse from all the yelling she'd been doing. "I'm Kate. I'm the conductor on this train."

The buzzing of the bees sounded like pain to her. It sounded like death. But Kate didn't run. If they could smell her fear, then she must be reeking of it.

But that was silly. As it had before, the sound shaped itself into words.

"I am bees!"

Kate hugged herself. She wondered exactly how many bees were in the car with her, and how many stingers were on all those bees, and how many gallons

of venom were in all those stingers, and how much venom it would take to kill an eleven-year-old girl.

"Are you sure you don't mean 'We are bees'?" She willed her voice to be steady. "That would be, you know, the regular grammatical way to say that."

"*Human grammar is not well suited to bees,*" the bees buzzed. "*There are lots of us, but we all think and act together, as one. Ergo, I am both singular and plural.*"

"Well. How about that."

Kate wiped her sweaty palms on her thighs. The bees sounded like they knew what *ergo* meant.

"I know you can't literally smell fear," she said, "but I should probably tell you that I'm really, really scared of you."

"*Actually, I can smell your fear. Bees communicate through smell in much the same way you do through sound. Our sense of smell is about a hundred times as strong as yours.*"

Huh.

"*You should know that human fear is very frightening to animals. People who are afraid are very unpredictable. They do dangerous things.*"

"Oh. I'm sorry about that. If it helps, I'm not

going to do anything at all. I'm just going to stand here."

"Good. I'm just going to keep doing what we do."

"Good. Great. It's a deal then."

She was still scared, but at least she hadn't run away. Yet. She wiped her forehead. It was pretty warm here in the garden car.

"I came in here because I was feeling bad. I don't know if you know about this, but humans have been causing a lot of problems lately. We made a lot of animals extinct. And we messed up the climate. We've killed a lot of bees, too, with pesticides and things like that."

"Yes. I know." The bees buzzed to themselves a little. *"You feel guilty and ashamed—we can smell that, too. You can't hide much from a bee."*

"I don't know how to make things better."

"But you have to try. Even if you don't know what you're doing half the time."

"More than half, if we're being honest."

"I was being generous."

At least her shame and guilt were helping her forget about her fear. For a while she just listened to the bees buzz and watched them coming and going, industriously visiting one flower after another. She made herself breathe deeply.

"Do you know how long it takes animals to evolve?"

Kate still didn't like having to guess things. So she waited, and the bees went on.

"A long time. It can take us a million years to evolve into something new. But it's different for humans. You can change quite quickly. You do it in a single generation sometimes, not by changing your bodies but by changing your minds. In that sense every generation of humans has a chance to be a completely new kind of animal.

"So who knows, your generation could be the one that changes everything. Remember that, when you feel despair. It's not impossible. You could be the ones."

That did make Kate feel better, a little bit. It was one of the very few hopeful things she'd ever heard anybody say that struck her as true and not wishful thinking.

"We might not change, though. We might not be the ones."

"I didn't say I wasn't worried. If you don't change, we're all in a whole lot of blazing trouble."

"I didn't know bees knew bad words."

"When you can smell as well as we can, you basically know everything."

"Really?" Kate said. "Like what else?"

"Like I know your friend Jag totally has a crush on you."

"Oh." She blushed. "I guess there are some things I would rather not know."

The bees made a rumbling sort of buzz that might almost have been bee laughter.

"Welcome to my world."

Happy Birthday

KATE HAD BEEN AWAY FOR SO LONG, AND SO MANY THINGS had happened to her, that by the time she got back home she'd almost forgotten what day she was supposed to be pretending it was. For a scary second she thought it might be her birthday, which ordinarily she loved. But she wasn't feeling in a very celebratory mood right now.

But she was spared all that because it wasn't her birthday, it was the day before her birthday. So she had time to tell everybody she had a headache and fall into bed and sleep for twelve hours before she had to wake up and turn another year older.

When she did, Kate was surprised at how much

she enjoyed it. Her parents had bought her favorite cereal, the one that was so irredeemably unhealthy that they only got it for her once a year, and they'd blown up a lot of balloons. They'd bought her a bunch of presents and also—by family tradition—a smallish present for Tom, so he wouldn't feel left out.

It was a funny little group that gathered that night for Kate's twelfth birthday dinner, at least from the point of view of Kate's parents. There were Kate and Tom, of course, but there was also Uncle Herbert, who had just reappeared after having been gone for four months with no plausible explanation whatsoever. Though Kate's dad did remark that wherever he'd been, he'd definitely lost some weight. There was also Tom's new friend, Wren, and Kate's new friend, Jag, whom they'd somehow failed to ever mention, which might have bothered their parents except that Jag had better manners than any kid they had ever seen, and most adults too.

And when the cake came out, everybody—with maybe the very slight possible exception of Kate—admired Jag's moving tenor rendition of "Happy Birthday," with ukulele accompaniment.

"I must say you're all in a pretty solemn mood," Kate's dad said when Jag was finished.

"It's my advanced age," Kate said. "I'm too busy contemplating my imminent death to celebrate another step in my inevitable journey to the grave."

"Stop being so morbid," her mom said—or started to say, because just then something in the window caught her eye. She froze. Then she made a mad dash for the back door, stopped, dashed back into the dining room, grabbed her phone, and sprinted out into the backyard.

"I hope she would take it as a compliment," Jag said, "if I said that I have never seen a woman of her age move that fast before."

"She ran track in high school," Uncle Herbert said proudly. "Hundred-meter hurdles."

When she came back, it was with an air of triumph. She held out her phone.

"Look!"

Everybody looked. It had a picture on it of a small, glittering green dragonfly.

And not just any dragonfly. It was a Hine's emerald.

"Can you believe it?" She was as happy as Kate had ever seen her. "It worked! We brought it back!"

Kate couldn't help smiling, too, for just about the first time all day. It had really worked. Her parents had rewilded their woods, or enough to satisfy an endangered dragonfly anyway. It was a tiny victory, just like the burying beetles. One tiny part of the world now worked just a little bit better than it had before.

She hugged her mom.

"That is the best birthday present you have ever gotten me."

"Well, you're welcome," her mom said. "But we got you a new bike, too, just in case."

After cake the four kids went out back to the *Silver Arrow*. It was twilight, and there were early fireflies out, winking on and off to each other in their mysterious silent codes.

"I wonder what's going to happen now," Tom

said. "I mean, with the railroad and the Board of Directors. What are they going to do to us?"

"I don't know." Kate had been wondering that, too. "We broke a lot of rules. I keep expecting to look out the window and see that the *Silver Arrow*'s gone."

TO BE COMPLETELY HONEST

I KEEP EXPECTING THAT TOO

"We'd still have the *Barracuda*."

THANKS A LOT

"*You'd* still have it, Skipper," Kate said. "It's not my submarine. Anyway, it's not much good without the *Silver Arrow* to take it places."

"Permission to come aboard?"

It was Uncle Herbert, calling up from the lawn.

"That's a naval expression," Tom called back. "Not suitable for use on trains."

"Well, what am I supposed to say if I want to get on a train?"

OH JUST GET IN

The *Silver Arrow*'s cab was getting crowded with five people in it, but Herbert didn't seem to mind. He climbed in, a little red-faced with the effort, and produced a thick creamy envelope from an inside pocket.

"From the board."

With a flourish he presented it to Kate. She eyed it nervously.

"Are we all fired?"

"Don't be dramatic. Just open it."

In the envelope Kate found an official timetable, with the fancy paper and the old-timey fonts and everything, just like she used to get. But where it would usually have had the list of dates and times and places it just said:

HAPPY BIRTHDAY

"Oh."

Kate let out a huge breath she hadn't realized she'd been holding.

"That's nice of them," she said in a small choked voice.

"I'll say," Uncle Herbert said. "I thought they were going to fire you!"

The timetable was more than a birthday card, it was also a gift, because it meant that at long last they were officially entitled to take the *Silver Arrow* out, and since there was no destination specified, they could go wherever they liked. So they did. Last year Kate's birthday had lasted about a month aboard the *Silver Arrow*, and she wasn't going to stretch this one out that long, but she decided she'd stretch it a bit. It was a tradition.

They started at the Rail Yard, where they picked up the cassowary and the wolverine and the rest of the train cars. Then they told the *Silver Arrow* to go wherever it wanted and went to sit in the library car, which was roomier than the cab.

The cassowary presented Kate with a magical birthday cake in the shape of a train that actually went around and around a little track. Kate had already had cake, but she ate a slice of the caboose to be polite. The cassowary had envelopes for them, too.

"First," she announced grandly, "each of you has received a letter of reprimand from the Board of

Directors for your reckless, unsanctioned, and wholly irresponsible activities."

She placed them on the library table.

"What about you?" Wren said. "You went along with it, too."

"I got a letter, too."

"So did I," the wolverine said. "I ate it."

Kate didn't eat hers, but she didn't bother to read it, either. She felt like she pretty much knew what it said. She balled it up and tossed it into the woodstove.

"Second," the cassowary said, "each of you has received a letter of commendation from the board for your resourceful, innovative, and entirely praiseworthy activities."

"Wait—really?" Kate said.

"Bit of a mixed message," said Jag.

"It comes with membership in the Order of the Silver Whistle." The cassowary placed a small wooden case on the table with her great gray foot. It contained four gleaming silver pins. "You wear them along with your regular conductor pins."

"What?!" Uncle Herbert said. "I've *always* wanted to be in the Order of the Silver Whistle!"

"You should've been more resourceful," Tom
said. "And innovative."

"And praiseworthy," growled the wolverine.

"I've never heard of it," Kate said. "What does it
mean?"

"It means you get to wear a pin!" Herbert said.
"You're also entitled to a special Order of the Silver

Whistle lounge car, but the pin is the main thing. It's also a whistle—look."

He picked one up and blew into it rather solemnly. It sounded exactly like a train whistle.

"You can have mine," Kate said.

"I don't want yours! I want them to give me one!"

Kate was relieved that he hadn't called her bluff. She liked her whistle pin.

"I have a present for you, too," Jag said.

"Really?"

"Come on. I'll show you."

He stood up and gestured gallantly for her to accompany him. Kate felt some trepidation, in light of what the bees had told her, but she went.

She figured he was heading for the ice cream car, which she was not particularly longing for after two rounds of birthday cake, but instead Jag stopped between two train cars and climbed the steel ladder that led up to the roof of the train.

Kate had been on top of the *Silver Arrow* before, but never while it was moving. She'd always meant to go, she'd just never quite gotten around to it, partly because she was a tiny bit scared. But Jag didn't seem scared, so when he reached down a hand to help her up, she disdainfully swatted it away.

In fact, it *was* scary up there—but not too scary. Without saying anything, she and Jag mutually agreed that standing up would've been a bit much, so they both sat cross-legged. The *Silver Arrow* was rolling smoothly across a wide grassy plain dotted with trees that cast huge, long shadows across the flat land. It was fun, whipping along with their hair blowing around.

"I always wanted to do this on the *Swift*," Jag said, "but it has solar panels on the roof."

"Really?" That sounded cool. Kate suppressed a pang of envy. "How is the *Swift*?"

"My dad says it'll be good as new."

They looked out at the view. The wind smelled deliciously of warm summer grass. Kate didn't know whether to feel happy or sad. First she'd thought they were going to solve everything; then she'd thought they'd ruined everything; and now she wasn't sure what she'd done. A bit of both, maybe. She still didn't know whether she was the hero of this story or the villain—but she supposed that was the difference between a story and real life. In real life nobody ever told you which you were. You had to figure it out for yourself.

The one thing she knew for certain was that whatever happened, they had to keep going. It wasn't enough to do nothing, it was too late for that. In her clumsy, stumbling human way, she had to keep trying to fix what was broken. In a world that was this out of balance, the biggest risk was not taking a risk.

And we can still change, she thought. *Like the bees said. Every year, every day, every second, we have the chance to change.*

"We can't give up," Jag said quietly.

Their thoughts must've been going in parallel. Kate nodded. "We can't give up."

The train went around a gentle curve, and she clung to the roof for dear life. She didn't understand how people had fistfights on these things in movies! But she had to admit it was nice sitting up here with Jag. It reminded her of being in the chorus—it was like the best part of her real life and her secret life, all mashed up together. It's all well and good to have a secret double life, but it's even better when there's someone else who knows about it, someone you can share it with. Even if that does make it a little less secret.

"You mentioned something about a present," she said cautiously.

"I did indeed."

"Jag, before you say anything else, I just want you to know that I'm really glad we're friends but—"

"I'm going to teach you how to sing."

"I—but—wait, what?"

Kate was relieved and then horrified all over again.

"I was there at your audition. You have an excellent voice. It's just a bit tentative. You have to learn to project. With some training you could do much better next year."

Jag had learned a few things about making friends, and maybe even about letting other people share the spotlight, but he could still ignore a social cue with the best of them.

"There's not going to be a next year," Kate said firmly. "I may be a human being, but I still like to think I can learn from my mistakes. There's no way I'm ever trying out for any theatrical production of any kind, ever again."

"We'll start with your breathing."

And he sang the first line of his big number, the duet that Hope Harcourt sings with Billy Crocker. It was catchy and tuneful, and the words were clever. Kate quite enjoyed hearing other people sing it.

"Now you."

"No!" Kate said. "This is not me! I don't do this!"

"A great woman once observed," Jag said, with just a trace of a smile, "that the most dangerous sentence in the English language is 'We've always done it this way.'"

Kate sighed. She knew who the great woman was. It was Grace Hopper, pioneering computer programmer and Kate's personal role model.

And was she really sure she couldn't do it? How did she know? She looked out at the great green world rolling past her and thought about the other hard things she'd done. She'd faced the most dangerous bird in the world, and an angry wolverine, and a speeding locomotive, and a submarine, and the Board of Directors of the Great Secret Intercontinental Railway. And a whole lot of elephants, and a bushfire, and her own failures, and the loss of a dear, dear friend. She'd faced all the troubles of the world, for good or for ill, and who wanted to face those?

Nobody. It was so much easier to look away. But Kate wasn't going to do that. She was going to make the hard choice instead and try to make things better. And if she could do that, what couldn't she do?

She closed her eyes, took a deep breath, and sang.